Burning

Book 3 in the Building Jerusalem series

David Flin

First published by David Flin, 2020
Copyright © 2020 David Flin
All rights reserved.

Cover artwork by Anastasia Nikolova

For further Books from
Sergeant Frosty Publications, please visit:

www.sergeantfrosty.com

Dedicated to:

Uncle Andrew. Always available.

Burning Gold.

The four of them settled down in a compartment on the train. Lieutenant Hawkins had told them the journey would take 24 hours and that NCOs would be coming along to check at regular intervals.

"Make sure you get plenty of sleep," he said. "There's no telling how much we'll get once we get there."

With that, he was gone, moving along the train. Thomas got out the well-worn playing cards and the four of them started playing bridge. Occasionally, Thomas looked out the window. They played until darkness fell. What he'd seen had been largely flat desert, with nothing much to look at. He wondered if it would be like that at wherever they were going to.

Probably not, he reflected. They would be on the train for 24 hours, so that meant wherever it was they were going to could be a thousand miles away.

From time to time, Frank went off to do his rounds of the train. From time to time, the train stopped at stations where food was available on the platform. Sergeant Taylor collected the food. The Riflemen weren't allowed to get off the train. "Riflemen is like puppies. They'll wander off and shove their noses into all sorts of mess. You keep them on the train, Corporal Barry."

The sun rose and it grew hotter and hotter in the train. "Wonder how hot it is out there?" Peter had asked, jerking his head towards the window. "Out there in the sun. Hotter than Hell, I reckon."

It was too hot to play bridge, so they tried to sleep. Thomas lay on the floor, head on his pack, but sleep was fitful. It was hot and there was no cooling breeze. He wasn't scared, he kept telling himself. He was just excited. He remembered how bored he had been before he joined the Army. He wasn't bored now. Was he wrong for feeling that the possibility of death made him feel more alive? Was he a thrill-seeker? Peter had told him of soldiers like that, who had relished taking risks. They never lived long.

"Be careful." Emily's words bounced around inside his head. Maybe hope was not lost.

The train rattled on, mile after mile. It entered mountainous terrain and climbed higher, although it didn't seem to get any cooler. Thomas saw people working in the fields. Men dressed in sombre blacks, women in bright reds and yellows, almost painfully bright as the sun caught them.

It was mid-afternoon when Lieutenants Hawkins and Campbell came along the carriage, calling in at each compartment.

"One hour to Esfahan," said Lieutenant Campbell cheerfully. "Have your tickets ready, along with your kit and yourselves." He sounded as excited as Thomas felt.

"Sir. Word, please," Frank said. He took Lieutenant Campbell to one side. "Sir, your job is to keep men calm, not get them excited."

"You're right, of course, Corporal. Cool of the evening, a nice little route march to the base, and then we'll see what will be our home for the next two years."

The troops disembarked from the train and a crowd watched them. No cheers, or shouts, or attempts at conversation. Just watchfulness. Thomas got the sense that they were wary and distrustful.

Lieutenant Campbell and Sergeant Taylor exchanged a look. The two Lieutenants spoke, while Sergeant Taylor called the men to attention.

"Corporal Barry. You command a section of your disreputables and the blacks. I want a steady corporal keeping an eye on the new and the unpredictable. Keep them steady." He stepped over and leaned down to speak so that only Frank could hear. "Your first command, lad. Just keep them steady. It'll never be this scary again."

A moment of waiting while Sergeant Taylor and Lieutenant Hawkins talked, glancing at the onlookers.

"Fix bayonets," Sergeant Taylor ordered. "Just a bit of display for the locals. Make sure we've got space to march. Plenty of swagger. Corporal Barry, make sure your section stays steady."

"Silence in ranks," said Frank, quelling the excited chatter of the new recruits. "Thomas, Charlie, you're buddies for the march. Windy and Davie. Peter and Edward. Abe and Billie. Keep things steady."

The troops headed out of the railway station, the sun starting to sink and the fierce heat starting to abate. Crowds lined the streets and the soldiers passed through what was obviously a poor area of the town. The crowds seemed to be in a sullen mood. Not aggressive, but distinctly unwelcoming.

They came to a long stone bridge across a sluggish river. A shop was busy closing at the base of the bridge, hurriedly boarding up as the riflemen approached. It seemed to be a teashop, but they were clearly not welcome there.

They felt as though there was an air of fear among the crowd.

The buildings on the other side of the bridge were clearly those of better-off people. The streets became broader. Then they heard shots fired ahead. Some distance off, but clear. The soldiers picked up their pace and Lieutenant Hawkins gave the order to deploy by sections, putting gaps between the four sections.

"We don't know what's coming," said Peter. "This means only one section falls into a trap. And we're at the front."

The firing grew louder as they drew closer, ragged individual shots. A plume of smoke rose into the air.

"Corporal Barry, take your section ahead, see what's going on. Observe and report. Wait for support."

"Thomas, buddy with Charlie. Peter, with Edward. Windy, you've got Davie. Abe and Billie, you're with me." Damn. He'd already told them that.

The section moved ahead at the double, seeing archways ahead, and flames through the arches.

"Peter, take point. Thomas, support. Windy, rear guard. Abe, Billie, stick with me."

They went through the nearest arch, hearts pounding as they did so. Once they were through, they fanned out into an arc. They looked out onto an enormous rectangular grassy park, with market stalls scattered around the park. The whole space was surrounded by a brick building with dozens of archways connecting the space with the outside world. At one end of the park, a dozen, maybe more, horsemen in uniform were riding around, shooting pistols into the air and sometimes at people trying to run away from them.

"Abe, Billy, run back to Lieutenant Hawkins. Tell him 15 cavalry in bazaar on rampage. Say it back."

"Fifteen cavalry in bazaar on rampage. Keep some for us."

"Spread out," Frank started to say.

"No," Peter said urgently. "Stay together. If we separate, we will get taken apart."

Observe, report, wait for support. Those were his orders. The crowd was fleeing about in all directions, panicking. The horsemen drove the crowd mercilessly, overturning tables, lashing out with long sticks, occasionally shooting into the crowd. A few tables were burning.

Observe, report, wait for support. The trouble was, the crowd was trying to flee the square, crowding towards the exits. That would make it hard for the rest of the platoon to get in.

"Grant, Miller, O'Grady. Load. Wait for orders."

"Frank," said Thomas pointing to where a horseman had thrown a rope around a civilian and was dragging him behind the horse.

"Blacks, you keep space clear so your buddy can shoot. Buddies, wait for order." The new recruits hadn't fired a rifle yet. They weren't to be trusted under these circumstances, but they could keep problems off the backs of the buddies so they could. Where was the platoon?

They could see the horsemen more clearly now. The horsemen were clearly out of control. Fifteen, Frank could count. Civilians were streaming past them towards the exits, the horsemen were shooting after them. Some of the shots were coming too close for comfort.

Where was the platoon? Frank was getting worried; he also knew he couldn't show any worry.

One of the horsemen looked straight at Frank, pointed a gun in his direction, then shifted the gun and shot a civilian.

He had to do something, or else the horsemen would start on them. "Buddies, one round over their heads."

The rifles barked and the horsemen pulled away in surprise, milling around at the far end of the square, some three hundred yards away.

Where was the rest of the platoon? A glance towards the arches told him that no-one would be coming in quickly against the crush of people trying to get out. It was going to be a very long few minutes before the platoon could arrive.

Sergeant Taylor would give him hell for opening fire.

The horsemen were gathering again. Frank could see them pointing angrily towards his section.

"Remember what I said. Blacks, keep people away from your buddy. If horse gets close, bayonet it. Thrust, twist, withdraw, like I taught you. Steady. We stay together. Stay together, we come through this."

The horsemen had reached a decision. They formed up into open order and drew swords. They started their horses towards the section at a walk.

"Steady, buddies. Steady, blacks. This might just be a scare."

One of the horsemen suddenly started a gallop. Frank heard Thomas mutter: "Too soon, the idiot." The other horsemen followed, the line now a ragged mess. They were waving swords and screaming.

"Steady." Frank tried to keep his voice steady as he remembered what Sergeant Taylor had told him. Let them come halfway, give them chance to veer away.

"Buddies, steady." Frank wondered how his voice was staying so calm. The horsemen were now a mob, all order gone. But the swords were pointing at the platoon.

Please let the rest of the platoon arrive.

One fifty yards, and no sign of turning aside.

"Aim for horses. Buddies only. Five rounds, independent fire."

*****

It had only lasted a few seconds. The horsemen had charged towards them. Thomas had been scared, and then the order to fire had come and it had been a matter of pick a target, aim, squeeze the trigger, feel the rifle kick against the shoulder, then pick another target. No need to think, just automatic. One shot was enough to bring down the target; it was hard to miss a target the size of a man on a horse.

He hadn't heard anything, which was strange given how much noise the rifles made. Now he could hear again, he could see something other than the view through the sight on his rifle.

The horsemen were fleeing, some on horse, some on foot. Those on foot were quickly swamped by civilians. Along the line, he saw a horse struggling to get to its feet near Windy and Davie, with Davie withdrawing his bayonet from the horse's rider.

"*Usuthu*," Davie seemed to be saying, but it was hard to tell. He certainly seemed pleased with himself, to judge by the exuberant way he was dancing and hugging Windy. Windy pushed him off, embarrassed, and Davie seemed to be puzzled about this.

"Stand ready," shouted Frank, trying to get the section back under control. It turned out that it wasn't actually necessary, then the rest of the platoon arrived. Frank breathed a deep sigh of relief.

"What was that all about, Corporal?" asked Lieutenant Hawkins. "Didn't I say wait for the platoon?"

"Sir, we come under fire, then attacked."

"We'll go through your report later, Corporal. Sergeant Taylor, stabilise the situation. What is it, O'Grady?"

"Sir, I've had basic medical training. Wounded civilians out there, Sir."

"Corporal Barry, three of the recruits to go with O'Grady. Make sure he doesn't get troubled by unfriendlies."

Thomas hurried across to the nearest body, with Abe, Billy, and Davie following. There wasn't a great deal he could do in many cases. Stop the bleeding where he could, cover up the faces of those where they were beyond help. One where he could stop extensive blood flow. A middle-aged woman, looking very pale.

Just focus on the wound, and deal with it.

*****

An old man with a long beard and a turban approached Lieutenant Hawkins. Frank busied himself with checking the equipment of his section, those who weren't tending the wounded, and making sure that the Lieutenant had a guard close by in case of further trouble.

"You will be staying here?" the old man asked, in poor and broken English.

"I have my orders," Lieutenant Hawkins replied stiffly, not wanting to give too much information. "Alasdair, keep the men together."

"They come often. They get drunk and come. Take what they like. Will you stay? Do you wish strong drink? Women?"

"My orders are to prepare the base for the Regiment." Lieutenant Hawkins looked around the bazaar, then back at the old man. "I must follow orders."

"They will return."

"It is too late to move to the base tonight. It is dark and we are not familiar with the route or the terrain. We will leave for the base in the morning. We will bivouac here tonight. How many cavalry are there? What forces? Are they bandits? Where are they based?"

"Not bandits. Army of Shah. They not paid for year."

Lieutenant Hawkins sighed. This was not a good start to the deployment.

*****

Davie stood guard over Thomas, while Abe and Billie found cloth for Thomas to use in his work. He had stopped the bleeding. The patient would have a scar down the length of their arm, but they'd live.

He stood up and started to move towards the next patient. He felt someone tugging at the sleeve of his jacket. He looked and saw a young girl, maybe aged eight or nine, slim, dark-haired, with large brown eyes. She held on to his sleeve and pointed at a body on the ground.

"Davie, keep her out from under my feet," Thomas said sharply. He knelt down to look at the body trapped beneath a fallen timber. He stood up again almost straight away. The woman had long since stopped breathing. He shook his head.

"Davie, find out what Lieutenant Hawkins wants to do with this girl."

Davie held his hand out for the girl to hold while they walked across to see Lieutenant Hawkins. She looked at the hand, puzzled. She then touched the back of his hand with a finger, and rubbed, seeing if the colour came off. He took her hand and rubbed the back of it with a finger. She giggled, then he giggled with her. They walked over to the Lieutenant.

"What is it?" Lieutenant Hawkins said, irritably.

"Sir, the girl lost her mother and father."

"That's a pity. What are we supposed to do about it?"

"Find her a home, Sir."

"Well?" Lieutenant Hawkins asked the old man.

"She is from south of river." The old man said it as though that should mean something. He looked at Lieutenant Hawkins and realised that it didn't. "The Armenians live south of the river." He paused again. "They are not Persian."

"Then take her south of the river and find her a home," Lieutenant Hawkins said. He had a lot to do, and this was just a delay.

The girl shook her head and held on to Davie's leg with both arms.

"Rifleman Davie, take her to Corporal Barry and get it sorted out. Sergeant Taylor. We'll be making camp here tonight. Sort out guards."

While Davie joined Frank and most of the rest of the section, Thomas reported to Lieutenant Hawkins.

"I've done what I can, Sir. I saved a couple, maybe. A couple didn't make it."

Lieutenant Hawkins nodded and told him to return to his section. "Oh, and O'Grady. Clean your jacket. It's filthy." He turned to speak to Sergeant Taylor about setting guards for the camp. It was going to be a long night for him.

*****

Thomas saw the girl sitting next to Davie while Peter tried to light a fire.

"What's going on? Isn't the tea ready?" He watched as Davie and the girl played a game. It seemed to involve one of them holding a hand out flat, palm down, while the other rubbed a finger on the back of the held-out hand, then they both giggled.

"What's that all about?" Thomas asked.

"They're seeing if they can rub the colour out," said Windy.

Frank sighed. "Hawk say we have to find home for her. She orphaned. She Armenian, so Persians not want her."

"Why on Earth not?" Thomas asked.

"Why do you think?" said Peter. "It would be like asking Lord Muck to adopt a kid from a State School. Here it's Persians and Armenians."

"Why don't the Armenians take her in?"

"Because she's lived with the Persians. That's why she's on this side of the river."

"Lieutenant Hawkins wants us to find her a home," said Windy.

"What's your name?" Thomas asked her. She looked blankly. He pointed at himself. "Thomas." He pointed at each of the others in the section and said their name.

She nodded and pointed to herself. "Hayastan. Hayastan."

"Where do you want to live, Hayastan?"

She looked at him blankly. He repeated the question in Persian, and she flung her arms around Davie. Davie stood up and she held on around his neck, the two of them laughing.

A thought struck Thomas. He'd been wondering how he could make things better for people who needed it. He needed to make a start somewhere and this looked like a good opportunity.

"The Persians don't want Hayastan. The Armenians don't. She's got no family. The answer is obvious."

"No," said Peter. "Whatever your idea is, it's a bad idea."

"What happened to solidarity among the proletariat?"

"Solidarity goes out the window when you start scheming."

"Hear me out. The Regiment is a family. We adopt her. Give her a home with us."

"How? We soldiers. It no place for child." Frank was more uncertain than he sounded.

Thomas played his winning argument. "When the wives get here it will be. Don't you think Joy would love to find out what having a child is like? Look how Hayastan gets on with Davie."

"Lieutenant Hawkins not be pleased." Frank was weakening. He knew Joy would love the idea.

"Well," started Thomas.

"We must tell Hawk. No trying to hide her. If we do this, we do it openly."

*****

"You and the recruits want to do what, O'Grady and Corporal Barry?" Lieutenant Hawkins seemed to be a little stressed.

Thomas spoke up. "Sir, are they recruits? They fought, stood with us. They did their job in battle. They're veterans. That's more than anyone in the other sections can say."

"They've not fired a rifle. We can't call them riflemen if they haven't fired a rifle." Lieutenant Hawkins sounded irritated.

"No, Sir. But we can't call them recruits when they're veterans of battle, Sir. Rifleman Recruit Davie managed to kill one of them and took down a horse. They've been through a battle, Sir."

"They might be veterans, but they aren't riflemen." Lieutenant Hawkins stated that with finality.

"Veteran Recruits, Sir?" suggested Thomas. "It will make them happy."

"It help us tell them apart from Persian recruits, Sir."

"Give me strength. Corporal Barry, these Zulus are black. The Persians won't be. It will be easy to tell a Zulu from a Persian."

"What if it's dark, Sir?"

"O'Grady, do you ever get the feeling that if you say one more word that's pushing the boundary, you'll incur my severe displeasure?"

"What's O'Grady scheming?" asked Lieutenant Campbell cheerfully.

"He wants the Regiment to adopt that orphan."

"Good idea," Lieutenant Campbell said. "Gives the women something to do straight away when they get here. It will help create a good impression with the locals, steadies the men – responsibilities always do that. You've got your hands full here, I'll supervise this."

*****

It was morning. Lieutenant Hawkins didn't expect it to be a good morning. There was bound to be fall-out from last night. The mayor, or whatever he was, had called again, asking for the platoon to stay in the city.

"Once the rest of the Regiment arrives, the Colonel will deal with the issue."

The Mayor hadn't been happy, but that was all he could do.

Then he had to try and keep Lieutenant Campbell in hand. Enthusiasm was all very well, but it had to be balanced with keeping the men steady. He would learn, if things didn't fall apart in the next five days.

Still, this was the whole point of the platoon. To go ahead of the Regiment and deal with unknown issues. That was why they'd taken on recruits who looked like they could show initiative and bring unexpected skills into the mix. The Zulus seemed to be a steady bunch. Damn good in close quarters, if Davie was anything to go by.

Riflemen shouldn't get into close quarters, but it was a skill and a valuable one at that. When you needed it, you needed it badly.

He worried about what the Persian recruits might be like. He was fairly confident they would be dead weight and training them was going to be a problem. This stuff about problems between Persians and Armenians was unexpected. He knew, just knew, that he'd get a mix for the company.

The men were formed up, ready to head off to the site for the base. That child was with Barry's section, and he had to decide whether or not to order them to leave her behind. The problems of having her along were going to be horrible. There was the possibility of combat. They might have to move quickly. There might be things a child shouldn't see.

On the other hand, the men seemed very attached to her, and it would be heartless to just abandon her.

"Corporal Barry, your men realise that there may be further troubles up ahead? We could end up in a growl and the girl in tow could hamper us."

"We will cope, Sir."

"Women in the camp is bad enough. Children are even worse. Children with the unit while on manoeuvres? It's just not on."

"Sir, if she stay here, she die. No one to look after her. If she come with us, she have a good chance." Frank was insistent.

Lieutenant Hawkins looked around the men, formed up and ready. "It's not her that I'm worried about. She's not our responsibility. We can't look after every waif and stray in the country. We're a regiment, not an orphanage."

"She is our responsibility," said Frank, solidly. When we march off, she will follow. If she with us, she come to no harm. Hayastan is mascot."

Lieutenant Hawkins tried Sergeant Taylor. He understood the balance here. "Thoughts, Sergeant?"

"Villages, Sir. When we pass farming villages, she'll prove to the locals we're not here to harm them. Why, other children may want to join. We could form a second company."

"Sergeant Taylor, I hope that is a joke. Women learning to shoot. Children as mascots. Where will this all end?"

"Look on the bright side, Sir. We haven't seen what our Persian recruits will be like."

*****

Just as they were about to march off, the mayor made one last attempt to persuade Lieutenant Hawkins to keep the platoon in the city.

"Imam, Sir," said O'Grady. "It's like a bishop."

"Thank you, O'Grady. Back in line."

The mayor – Imam – explained that the city would like the platoon to stay. "How much?" he asked.

Lieutenant Hawkins sniffed. "We're not for sale. We'll be here regularly to keep an eye on things."

The mayor didn't seem happy, but he accepted the decision. With that, the platoon marched off, heading northwards. The flat farming land quickly gave way to more mountainous terrain, with the route winding through valleys. Hayastan walked alongside Davie, and she was learning a few English words. Her favourite phrase was: "Isn't it time for a bloody brew-up?"

When she got tired, Davie picked her up and she rode on his shoulders.

They passed a couple of small villages, a dozen stone buildings clustered together along the road, with tracks running from them up into grass-covered hills. "Shepherds," said Lieutenant Campbell, confidently. The doors were firmly locked, there was no sound from within the buildings, and no-one approached the soldiers.

The platoon had barely got warmed up, maybe five miles out from the city, when they came onto a flat plain halfway up the side of a hill. A steep hill to the east, a grassy plain almost billiard table flat stretching a mile to the west and ending in a steep slope down. North to south, about two miles, with a down slope to the south, and an up slope to the north. In the northeast corner, a small lake, fed by a river from the hills. Lieutenant Hawkins ordered a rest. While the men rested, he looked the site over with Lieutenant Campbell.

"Good site," Lieutenant Hawkins said. "Not the one we were told about. Is the ground hard enough for airships to come in?"

"Airships aren't heavy. Where's the problem?" asked Lieutenant Campbell.

Corporal Barry coughed. "Sir, they heavy when they let air out."

"And you know about this, how?" asked Lieutenant Hawkins.

"In London, Lady Dalkeith take us to see airships, learn about them, Sir."

"Of course. Obvious. Stupid of me. Check the ground to see if it's firm enough for airships, as you're the expert, Corporal." Lieutenant Hawkins looked around the site. "We'll need to check the other site, but this looks good. We're, what, five miles from the city? Water supply assured. Can you see any possible problems?"

"Weather," said Lieutenant Campbell, promptly. "Does it get snowed in during the winter? What about rains? Does anyone own it? Is the water supply clean?"

"Well done, Alasdair. That trail up the hill will make a good training ground for your screw-guns. And for defaulters. Wouldn't fancy running up there in full kit."

"Oh, I don't know. Bet there's a good view from the top."

"Only one way to find out, Alasdair. Take a couple of men. O'Grady needs the exercise. Tire him out. One of the Zulus. See if they can cope with physical exercise."

*****

Thomas wasn't used to being the only one out of breath. Abe had climbed up the slope like a goat, and Lieutenant Campbell casually told him that it was very like the hills on his father's estate. It was about a hundred miles to the top, Thomas thought. They'd climbed and scrambled and, in Abe's case, ran up the slope for half an hour. A hundred miles at least. Maybe a thousand miles.

But at least they could look around. The view was impressive. Miles in all directions.

"I rather think we could fire one of the screw-guns from here," Lieutenant Campbell said. "Trouble is, if we fire it across the flat bit, we would hit part of the camp. Still, it will be good exercise, carrying the guns up here. Fancy giving it a go, O'Grady?"

Thomas tried to think of an appropriate way of answering the Lieutenant that wouldn't get him into trouble. He looked around for inspiration and found it to the north. A cloud of dust moving along a track from the north, maybe twelve miles away. He pointed it out to Lieutenant Campbell.

"Cavalry at the walk," he said. "Veteran Recruit Abe. My compliments to Lieutenant Hawkins. Tell him cavalry approaching from the north. Maybe one hour away. They're in some force. Quick as you can, but make sure you get there safely. If you tumble and break your neck, the message won't get through. Off you go."

Abe hared off down the slope, and Alasdair looked towards the cloud. "It's a good vantage point, this. They're not moving quickly. Definitely a walk."

"How do you know that it's cavalry, not just shepherds, or something? Sir."

"Something they teach you in the dragoons. Scouting is what they do. Size of cloud, density, the way it's moving. Steady movement along the route means it's not animals. Infantry moves slower, much more compact. Length means that it's one, possibly two companies. All very basic. There's a second column behind the first. See how more compact that one is. Infantry. Large company size."

Thomas was impressed.

"Right. Scurry down, tell Lieutenant Hawkins that there's infantry following. I see our Zulu friend has passed on the glad tidings. Off you go. I'll check for further intelligence, then follow. Don't break your neck."

*****

The five sections formed up, four in a line in front, and Frank's section behind the line. Lieutenant Hawkins stood in the centre and waited. Thomas reached the base of the hill and rushed over to report to him.

"Very good, O'Grady. I'll need a runner. You're it. Here they come. Lieutenant Campbell, now that you're back, I'm going to speak with their commander. If I don't come back, assume that they're hostile." He started to walk forward, and Thomas followed him, feeling very exposed.

"Cheer up, O'Grady. If this goes bad, you'll know nothing about it. Keep your wits about you. I've a feeling I may need them."

Cavalry came out onto the plain from the track to the north. They came in file, then struggled to form a line.

"Not very good, are they," Lieutenant Hawkins said conversationally. "We'll wait here." They were about two hundred yards ahead of the platoon. "Sergeant Taylor knows how far I've come. You've been promoted to range marker, O'Grady."

Four riders came forward from the line of the cavalry. Two officers, one seemingly of high rank, and two NCOs.

"Notice anything about the cavalrymen, O'Grady?"

"Horses are in poor condition, Sir."

"What else? Come on, the platoon is going to be doing a lot of scouting. Notice details, O'Grady."

"The uniforms look odd. Some of them are different. Probably different units. Or they've been borrowing jackets."

"O'Grady, something really important. Something that makes a difference on the battlefield. The fact that they're not used to each other is important, but this thing is major."

Thomas looked carefully. They were having difficulty forming a line. The leather work was grubby and looked like it might be in bad condition. Sabres at the side, not drawn.

"No firearm, Sir."

"Finally, O'Grady. Here comes the entourage. Keep your mouth under control, or so help me, when we get back, you'll be in trouble."

The horsemen approached and Thomas got a closer look at the senior officer. Bespectacled, which surprised Thomas. Arrogant air about him. Annoyed look on his face.

"Are you the British officer?" he asked in accented English.

"Lieutenant Hawkins, Company Commander, First Battalion, Rifle Brigade."

"My men are very unhappy with you," the officer said. He sounded more petulant than authoritative.

"To whom do I have the honour of speaking?" Lieutenant Hawkins said.

"I am Sarhang Sardar Mofakham. I am an officer in command of the Army in this region. What were your troops doing last night?"

"You know, I rather think that I don't report to you. Your men appear to have come onto the site of our base of operations. Inadvertently, I'm sure."

"Your base of operations? I will have to check to see if we will permit that. My men are unhappy because they were assailed last night in the city. The villains in your unit will be handed over to us for discipline."

"No. My troops, my command, and our base. You are on our base without permission. I must ask you to leave. Otherwise, my orders are clear. So are my fields of fire. However," Lieutenant Hawkins said, drawing breath. "As per the agreement between our governments, we are here to support the Persian Government. This plateau is provisionally agreed as our base of operations. If I were you, I would check the agreement."

"And last night in the market square?"

"My men dealt with a disturbance caused by drunken bandits. They couldn't possibly have been dealing with soldiers. Four rifles dealt with it and didn't take a scratch. They'd have been in trouble if they had been facing real soldiers. As I understand things, we have been asked to support your government in maintaining law and order in the region, dealing with bandits wherever they might happen to be in the country. I believe you have similar objectives. We are therefore operating in parallel. I'm sure my Colonel will want to discuss matters with your commanding officer."

"You are hardly in position to take such an attitude. You should ask forgiveness, or my men will ride over you."

"Give the order to your men, by all means. I think we're done here, O'Grady."

As they walked back to the line, Thomas could hear the officer shouting at the cavalry. Thomas started to turn his head to look behind him.

"Eyes front, O'Grady. We'll see if anything is happening behind us from what our men do. This cavalry don't want to mix it up. We'll see how much control that officer has over them. But if you start looking behind you, you're liable to fall over and that might change the mood. So, head up, walk sensibly, and don't fall over."

They reached the line and Thomas was finally able to look back to the Persian forces. The cavalry was stubbornly standing still. Some infantry had come up. The officer was shouting, and the soldiers weren't paying any attention to him.

"They don't fancy it," said Lieutenant Campbell.

"They've got used to fighting civilians," Lieutenant Hawkins replied. Then he sighed. "We're going to be busy for the next few days."

*****

Frank spent the morning teaching the Veteran Recruits how to shoot. They were keen, but far too eager to run before they could walk. They wanted to learn the next step before they had mastered the first. Abe seemed less excitable than the others, and there was something vaguely familiar about some of Abe's gestures, but Frank couldn't work out what it was.

Two of the other sections stood on guard at the north and south end of the plain, where the routes entered. The other two relaxed until it was time to relieve a guard section. Peter and Windy kept watch from Lookout Hill, as they'd named it.

Hayastan watched the recruits training with the rifles, until she got bored of this. Then she started following Thomas around.

Thomas measured out spaces and tried to imagine where the buildings should go. Something nagged at the back of his mind, but he couldn't put his finger on what it was.

"What happened to your father?" he asked Hayastan, practising his Persian.

"He went away. He said he would come back, but Mother said he wasn't coming back." She gulped. "He's not coming back, is he. He's been killed. Now Mother has gone away. She's dead as well." She started to cry, great gulping sobs and she clung tightly to Thomas. "Why did they have to die?"

Thomas held her, but he didn't know what to say. He had no idea how to make this better.

"What was wrong with me? Why did Allah let them be killed?" Hayastan asked through tears.

"They are watching you, to see that you have a happy life. They will wait for you."

"Why did they leave me here alone?" Hayastan wailed.

"But they didn't. You've got us."

"You were sent, weren't you?"

"Well, we're part of the Regiment. We were told to come here," Thomas admitted.

"That means you were sent here. You spoke to Mother before she died."

Thomas didn't want to say that her mother had died before he got to her. "I spoke to her," he said, phrasing his words carefully.

"You spoke to her, and she is now in Paradise, and you were sent. Nine of you," she said, almost in awe. "You're my angels."

"We're not angels," Thomas said.

"You came from far away. You fought against the devils in the bazaar. You saved someone's life, and you spoke kind words to Mother as you sent her to Paradise. You're angels."

"We're not angels. We're just men."

"Well, you're *my* angels."

Thomas found it difficult to speak.

*****

Lieutenant Hawkins checked on how Thomas was getting on with the planning. "It looks perfect," he said. "We'll have to check on the intended site, but this looks ideal."

"Yes, Sir. Perhaps too much so."

"Devious mind working overtime, O'Grady? Care to explain?"

"If this place is so perfect, why is there nothing here? There's no village here. The Persian Army's not using it. There's no sign of bandits. Nothing. If it's so perfect, why isn't someone else using it?"

"I'm not interested in superstitious nonsense. There's no pathway to another world, the entrance to the Underworld isn't here."

"What if it's a holy place for the locals? They might get upset."

Lieutenant Hawkins paused and considered this. "You've got a point, O'Grady. We'll ask the Mayor tonight."

"Ask the Imam tonight, Sir?"

"Yes. We'll check the original site, then we're going back to Esfahan."

"Yes, Sir." Thomas sounded uncertain. "That's not what we expected, Sir."

"That's the point, O'Grady. No-one is expecting us to do that. The problem with dealing with bandits is getting to grips with them. You need to take them by surprise. Take them when they're not expecting you to be there."

*****

They moved off again, heading north towards the original site. The route wasn't very smooth. It was pitted, with small stones constantly shifting underfoot. Although the views were pretty, the path needed careful negotiation with steep slopes and treacherous footing.

"This would need levelling and improving," Lieutenant Hawkins said. "Easy enough to block this route off."

Naturally, the route didn't follow a straight line. It looped around; it went up and down. Rocks of varying sizes strewn along the way made travel along the route heavy going.

"This is obviously not going anywhere," said Lieutenant Campbell.

"Aside from the base assigned to us."

"What I meant was if there was anywhere that people lived, this would be a better route."

They climbed up another rise, then looked down on what looked like an abandoned ancient stone village. The stone was bright yellow, catching the sun in a glare. Lieutenant Hawkins called a halt and studied the village through binoculars. Not so much a village as a small town. Buildings cramped together, in a state of disrepair. Surrounded on three sides by steep hills.

"Sun trap in summer," said Lieutenant Campbell. "Death trap all year round. And something's not right here."

"He's right, Sir," said Sergeant Taylor. "Smells like a kill zone."

"No birds," Lieutenant Campbell said.

"If I were turning this into a death trap, where would I position my forces?" Lieutenant Hawkins mused. "There's a lot of hard cover in the village."

"No, there isn't," said Lieutenant Campbell. "It's old stone. No cover at all."

"How do you mean?"

"Lob in a shell. Old stone turns into instant shrapnel."

"Back packs down," said Sergeant Taylor.

The platoon made a small pile of their packs. Thomas picked the girl up. "Hayastan, you stay here. Look after these. We'll be back for them."

Sergeant Taylor inclined his head. "There's a man over by that double-pronged rock on the hill, near the tree. Another beside him. Bandits or soldiers?"

"Whichever it is, we're the only people who'd walk into there. This is too neat a trap for the soldiers we've seen," Lieutenant Campbell said.

"What do bandits have to gain?" Sergeant Taylor asked. "How would they know we were on our way here? And why buy trouble? Head back, Sir?"

"We're here to deal with bandits. Once the Regiment arrives, bandits will turn tail at the first sign of us. This is where we set the tone. If they're bandits, they're legitimate targets. If they're soldiers, they're not wearing uniform and they're acting like bandits. Sheepskin coat on that one. They're no soldiers. No-one's supposed to be here, so anyone here is up to no good." Lieutenant Hawkins weighed up the ground.

"Sir," asked Frank. "If they bandits, how they know we're coming here? And if they know, why stay here and not get far away?"

"Because right now, they've got the advantage over us. When the Regiment arrives, things are going to be hard for them. They've got to make a statement. How did they know? Someone told them. This is what we're going to do. Sergeant Taylor, take Section 1 back and around, find a way up to the top there. You should get a clear line into their backs. Quiet as you can, until you're in position. If there's opposition, use your judgement. You'll kick things off when you're ready."

"Not me, Sir?" asked Lieutenant Campbell. "I know hills."

"No, Alasdair. We'll need you when the screw-guns get here. You've got Section 2. They're our best shots. Find some cover, keep an eye out for where any shooting comes from. Shoot at nothing above that boulder where sheepskin currently is. Sergeant Taylor, that's your stop line. Lower than that, and you're at risk from us. Section 3 is the fastest, so will be in reserve. I'll command it. Section 4 will be with it. We'll wait here and see where we're needed. Corporal Barry, take your Section down towards the village. Stop one hundred yards from the first house, then start having a brew up. Make noise. They'll be watching you. When things kick off, deal with anything in the village. No-one is to enter any building on their own. Questions?"

"Kill or capture?" Frank asked.

"Don't take risks. It's going to be tough taking one back to the city for questioning. Don't worry about any fleeing the scene. They may be luring you into an ambush."

*****

It wasn't a comfortable brew up. They kept getting up and walking around, talking nonsense. The Zulus were excited, and it was hard work keeping them back.

"Same buddies as bazaar, OK?" said Frank.

Thomas glanced back, where he could just see the packs piled up around the corner. Hayastan was there.

"How long do you reckon they'll take?" He didn't need to say who 'they' were. "The bandits must be started to wonder what we're up to."

Abe started to point, and Frank snapped at him not to. "Don't point. Tell. If you point, they see."

"Sheepskin coat man moving."

They looked, and the man had stood up, rifle slung over his shoulder. He held his arms outstretched like a scarecrow.

"Keep eye elsewhere. Could be distraction. Keep watch elsewhere."

The man walked slowly down the hill towards the Section.

"Windy, keep him covered. Just covered. I think he wants to talk," said Thomas.

The man kept his arms outstretched.

"He's got guts, that's for sure. Should I meet him part way, Frank? Stop him seeing our dispositions." Thomas' heart was pounding.

"You take care."

Thomas stood up and slung his rifle, held his arms outstretched, then walked slowly towards the man. "What do you want?" he called in English.

"Talk," the man replied in Persian.

The two walked slowly towards each other, stopping when they were five paces apart. Close enough to make it a harder shot for anyone trying to hit one and not the other, far enough apart that there would be a brief warning if either tried brawling.

The man was average height, barrel-chested, with a thick, dirty beard. Thomas could smell him from this distance and wouldn't want to get closer. "Salam," he said quietly.

The man looked surprised. "Salam aleikom."

They looked at each other in silence for a moment.

"I am Thomas O'Grady."

"I am Antar al-Mulk. It is as good a name as any."

The two stared at each other, weighing each other up. Finally, Thomas spoke in Persian. "What are you doing here?" It was hard work interrogating someone in a foreign language.

"Hunting wolves. I am a shepherd."

"Really? Are all your friends also shepherds hunting wolves?"

The man smiled. "Persian wolves are very fierce. There are no wolves here, so my friends leave. Why are you here?"

Thomas struggled with the words. Should he tell the truth and say that it was because he was ordered here, and he didn't have a clue why? Maybe not. "To bring peace to a troubled land."

Antar's eyes flashed with anger. "It is soldiers who bring the troubles and break the peace. They loot and rob and kidnap and rape. They call those who fight back bandits."

Peter would love this, Thomas thought. "We are here to bring peace. Those who wish peace have nothing to fear from us."

"If it is *your* peace. The girl by your packs. She is not a soldier, I think."

"No. She is an orphan. We are looking after her."

"She is Armenian." Antar's voice was as emotionless as he could make it.

"She is a child. Would Allah look with favour on any who brought harm to an innocent child? The plain along this road. It is not used. Why is that?" Thomas wanted to get a few answers.

"Because the King wants it, the Governor wants it, and neither want the other to have it. That is what I say, but then again, I might be lying."

Thomas tried not to smile. "You are a devious, tricky, rogue," he said. He wondered if this was how other people felt when talking to him?

The man didn't bother to hide his smile. "Thank you. I think my other shepherds have left. I think you will not find many bandits who don't wear uniform."

"If we need a shepherd to help protect the innocent, I shall leave a message on this very spot."

They parted and Thomas returned to the Section. Lieutenant Hawkins was waiting.

"What the hell do you think you were playing at, O'Grady?"

"Scouting, Sir. He knew things."

"Did he speak English?"

"No, Sir."

"Then how did you talk to him?"

"French, Sir. It's very common in Persia." For the life of him, he didn't know why he told that lie. Well, not strictly a lie. It is very common in Persia. He wanted to keep the fact that he knew the language secret, because that way he could listen to private conversations. That must be the reason.

As they headed back, Thomas told Lieutenant Hawkins what he had learned.

*****

It was early evening when they got back to the city. The people watched them, uneasily. As they drew closer to the bazaar, the people they passed became silent and made sure they kept their stalls between themselves and the Riflemen.

"Send out a scouting section, Sir?" Sergeant Taylor asked.

"No. Too much chance of it getting isolated by screaming civilians. If there's nothing there, then there is no need for the scouts. If there's something there, they'll be isolated without being able to get a report back. Make sure the rifles aren't loaded. I don't want any chance of an accidental discharge." He had worried about this, but it would be an instant to load. He hoped that instant wasn't going to be vital. But an accidental discharge could lead to huge problems.

They passed beneath one of the arches. Stalls either side, and a door in each arch. Worth checking out in the morning. It wasn't relevant now, but it might be later.

The sections turned left and right either side of the arch, with Lieutenant Campbell between the two Sections to the left. Lieutenant Hawkins was with the three to the right.

There were about 50 Persian soldiers, mostly infantry, in the centre of the bazaar. These suddenly stood very still. They looked at the platoon, edged closer together, and tried to pretend they hadn't been shouting at the stall keepers.

"Corporal Barry, your Section will have fifteen minutes to look at the bazaar and make any purchases you want. Show those Persian soldiers how it's done. Return on my signal, then Section 1 will have a chance to do likewise. Section 1 and 2, stand easy. Section 3 and 4, stay on watch."

The Section looked at each other, then teamed up in their normal buddy pairs. Hayastan looked up seriously at Thomas. "I will go with Angel Davie. He will need my help talking to people. Is that all right, Angel Thomas?"

Thomas nodded, and she ran over to Davie and Edward, and stood between them, holding each of them by the hand.

The Persian soldiers watched them carefully and warily.

"We buy something for girls," Frank said. "What girls like?"

"Jewellery, clothes, perfume, stuff like that," Thomas said, watching Hayastan. Davie pointed to some fruit on a stall, and the stall owner said something. Hayastan shook her head and showed four fingers. Davie then held up four fingers. The stall owner said something else. Hayastan shook her head again and held up five fingers, and Davie held up five fingers. The stall owner reluctantly nodded, and Davie handed over five small coins. The stall owner accepted them suspiciously but didn't argue.

Thomas turned his attention to the Persian soldiers. They were watching both the Section and the Section standing watch. The Persian soldiers didn't look very happy.

"They don't know what to do," Thomas said.

"I not know either," Frank said. "This tablecloth nice."

"For crying out, Frank. You do *not* want to buy that for Joy."

"But it nice. It useful."

"Haven't you *ever* bought things for a lady? You do not buy something useful. How about this shirt thing?" He held up a white silk shirt, elaborately stitched with red patterns.

"It too small. Very flimsy, not wear well. Joy not like it."

"Trust me, she'll like it. She'll like the part where you help her put it on and, more importantly, help take it off."

Frank coloured. "She not like that."

"Trust me, she will."

Frank saw a handsome-looking pen. "She like to write. I take this."

Thomas saw a book. He recognised the name, but reading it was going to be hard. "Rubaiyat of Omar Khayyam. Why not?"

Frank snatched it from him. "Buy together. Get better price than separate." He held the two items out and asked the stall owner: "How much?"

The stall owner looked blankly at him. Thomas had a thought, then looked at the Persian soldiers, who were still huddling together. He pointed at one and then curled his index finger in a summoning gesture.

"What are you doing?" Frank asked.

"Building bridges. Maybe burning them." He pointed to the man and repeated the summoning gesture, then pointed to the ground next to him at the stall. The man looked around him desperately and his comrades took a step away from him. Thomas repeated the gesture, and the soldier took a reluctant step forward. Thomas repeated the gesture firmly. Eventually, the soldier stood on the spot Thomas had indicated.

The soldier's uniform was grubby, the buttons mismatched. The rim of the bayonet scabbard was rusty. Three days of stubble. Thomas shook his head. "This is what we'll be getting as recruits? God help us." He looked the soldier up and down. "This is what will happen," he said in Persian. "Stall man will tell you how much he wants. You tell me what he said. I tell the Corporal. The Corporal then tells me what he's prepared to pay, I tell you, you tell him, and we keep going until they both say the same amount."

"You speak Persian?" Frank asked.

"Yes. Don't tell anyone. If the officers realise, I'll be doing dangerous stuff." Thomas turned to the soldier. "Why you come here to cause trouble?"

"No pay, more than year. We only hurt peasants."

Thomas looked hard at him, and the soldier seemed to shrivel up. He'd said something wrong, and he felt very alone here.

Frank and the stall keeper finally agreed on a price. "We not have local money," Frank said.

"Peter, bring your kit over here." Once Peter arrived, Thomas smiled. "To each according to their need, isn't it? I need some of the stuff you lifted from the ship."

"Why?"

"To get stuff."

Peter was reluctant but parted with four strips of cloth with the name of the troopship on it.

"Naval cap tallies?" Thomas asked. "Why did you lift these?"

"Because I thought I might need them to give to you for some ridiculous trade in the middle of bloody Persia where ship tallies are of no conceivable use just so you can buy something for your girls, and I end up with nothing."

"You must be psychic," said Thomas. Thomas spoke to the stall owner. "Something for this soldier," he said, indicating the Persian. He had no idea if it would do any good, but it couldn't hurt.

*****

They'd finished making their purchases. Davie lay down to look at the stars and Hayastan curled up next to him and went to sleep. The other soldiers showed off to each other what they'd managed to buy.

A man asked Lieutenant Hawkins some questions and the Lieutenant glanced at Thomas. Thomas rose to his feet and headed over and almost saluted. A glare from the Lieutenant stopped him.

"Sorry, Sir. Force of habit."

"This gentleman heard that you helped the wounded last night."

Thomas looked at the man. Persian, maybe early 30s. Slim, tall, very clean. Looked clever, looked honest, looked dedicated.

"Is there a problem, Sir?" Thomas asked Lieutenant Hawkins.

"No problem," the man said, in very slow, very careful English. "I am a doctor. Doctor Hassan Hashemi. I wish to thank the man who gave aid to the wounded. It was a good thing to do." He turned to Lieutenant Hawkins. "When the rest of your people come, I would like to talk with your medical officer. I am sure we have much to learn from each other."

Thomas didn't like the man. He wasn't sure why.

*****

The Persian soldiers prepared to go back to their base. They had given no trouble in the bazaar. The platoon prepared to bivouac for the night.

"Corporal Barry," Lieutenant Hawkins said. "Are your men ready for a night patrol? Your mascot will have to stay here. Lieutenant Campbell will take care of her. He's getting married, he needs the practise."

"They ready. Where we go?"

"Those Persian soldiers are going back to their base. I want to know what their base is like. Can you manage that? No fighting. You're scouting, no more. Once you start fighting, you've made a mess of things. The trick is not to be seen."

"You want us go into base?"

"No. You're bound to be seen. You're collecting information. We want you to bring it back."

Frank raised the obvious point. "They our allies. We spying on our allies?"

"Exercising. It's an impromptu training mission. It's not that I don't trust them, but I don't trust them. Don't get seen."

Frank returned to the Section and told them they were going out on a night patrol. "It important we not get seen. Need to black up."

The Zulus looked confused.

"Boot polish on face, make face dark so it not show up at night."

The Zulus just looked at each other. Then Frank finally realised the problem. "Skin can show reflection, so even blacks need black up," he explained.

He would have got away with it if Thomas hadn't said: "Quick thinking."

*****

The trick was to be far enough away that you weren't seen by anyone glancing around, keeping absolutely quiet. Frank had remembered to check each man to make sure nothing jangled on their body. He had made them jump up and down to see if anything loosened and made a noise. He also had to be close enough to keep them under observation.

Frank was with Abe and Billy directly behind the Persians; Windy, Peter and Davie were off to the right, on the flank of the Persians; Thomas, Charlie and Edward to the left. They took great care not to be seen.

They didn't need to take such elaborate precautions. The soldiers weren't looking around, simply plodding along. There didn't seem to be any defensive patrols out. They followed a good road for a couple of hours, then the Persians turned on to a smaller road. As soon as they had done so, Frank and the others could smell the base. The strong smell of horse was unmistakeable. The stench of a lot of men living on a site was also strong.

The section went to ground and moved cautiously forward so that they could see into the base. Woods on two sides, open ground on this side and to the east, where the main road ran. The base consisted of dozens of large wooden huts, built on stone piles to keep them clear of the ground. A large number of stables and to one side, what looked like a canvas-covered dining area.

The two other groups had joined Frank and together they looked down from the slight rise into the camp. A single gate in, with a guard post.

"Count the stables, Abe, Windy. Count them separately. Davie, Billie, count the living huts, separately. Peter, Edward, look for officer quarters. Charlie, you keep an eye out for anyone coming this way. Thomas, you look at the fence around the base."

An eight-foot-tall fence surrounded the base, topped with wire. Possibly barbed wire, impossible to tell from this distance.

"It bends the wrong way," Thomas said, puzzled. "The wire. It leans in, not out."

"It's to keep people in, not out," Peter said.

Frank tried to count how many troops the base was intended for. About twice the space for horses as the dragoons had had on that training exercise in England. Maybe two regiments of cavalry. Housing for twice that number, so two regiments of infantry. Maybe.

Officers' quarters in the centre of the camp. There was one ornate building that no-one could work out what its function was. It was larger than any other building, more ornate, and with a guard at the door. As they watched, a young man in the uniform of a very senior Persian Army officer stepped out, along with two Europeans in uniform.

They shook hands outside the door, and the Europeans then walked to a large car. They opened the boot, took out a medium-sized suitcase, opened it and showed it to the Persian. They closed the suitcase and handed it to the Persian. They then got into the back of the car, which drove away.

"Damn," said Peter. "We'd best get back with this news."

*****

"Damn. I hate politics and diplomacy," said Lieutenant Hawkins. Thomas wisely refrained from saying that he'd noticed.

"What nationality were these Europeans?" Lieutenant Hawkins asked.

Frank wanted to shrug. "It dark, Sir." He was feeling annoyed. His Section had done a good job and Lieutenant Hawkins was ignoring this. "Hard to see details of uniform."

"People who'd bribe the Persian Army are up to no good, Sir," said Thomas.

"Amazing deduction, O'Grady." Lieutenant Hawkins' voice dripped with sarcasm.

"Yes, Sir. The French want this region quiet, Sir. They don't want things spilling over into their sphere. Italians have no interest here. Austrians have more than enough problems at home. They weren't Turkish. Too far for Spain. Unlikely to be American or Japan. Sweden's too busy calling its people home. Only really leaves Germany and Russia, and we know they've both been meddling here before, Sir."

Frank looked at Thomas with some awe. Lieutenant Hawkins was also impressed, despite himself. "How do you know all that, O'Grady?"

"Newspapers on troopship, Sir."

"I'm going to have to speak with this Persian commander. You want to say something, O'Grady?"

"Yes, Sir. Might be worth speaking to the Imam. If anyone knows what's going on, he should."

"You might have a point. Come on, then, O'Grady."

"Me, Sir?"

"Yes, you. You seem to understand this place. Must be all this Irish blood in Persia."

"Sir?"

"I'm surprised, O'Grady. Even I've heard of the famous Irish-Persian poet."

"Sir?"

"O'Mar Khayyam."

*****

"Don't look glum, lad," Sergeant Taylor said to Frank. "He didn't praise your work because you've reached the standard he expects. You've come a long way."

*****

Frank returned to the Section, which was grabbing some sleep before the day started. Hayastan was dragging one of the packs to a pile of the others.

"What you do, Hayastan?"

She stopped pulling the pack, which had been far too heavy for her to carry, and looked up at Frank, concentrating on the difficult words. "It is my job, Angel Corporal Father Barry. I look after packs when down packs."

"You show me where this go, I carry this one for you," Frank said.

"Then will it be time for bloody brew-up?"

*****

The Imam met them in a small room overlooking the bazaar. The windows were covered with a wooden shade, a fretwork that allowed light in while keeping the heat out. The Imam motioned for Thomas and Lieutenant Hawkins to sit at a table, while a young woman brewed tea by an oil stove.

"Excuse, please, the product of theft," the Imam said. On seeing the puzzled expression of his guests, he explained further. "Tea plants were from India, but some were smuggled out."

"We'd best drink the evidence," Lieutenant Hawkins said.

The woman placed the tea on the table and sat beside the Imam. She kept her head lowered when Thomas looked at her. She wore a dark scarf over her hair. Thomas couldn't see much of her, but she seemed to be about twenty. Long, dark hair, slim build, with long, slender fingers. Pianist fingers, his father had called them. She looked without moving her head and Thomas looked into large, dark-brown eyes filled with intelligence and mischief.

He decided to concentrate on his tea.

"Mayor, the plain five miles north of the city, lake in the corner. Are there any problems with our base being there?"

"There are reasons against it. Shah Qajar claims that it is his and he wishes to build a Winter Palace there. The Governor claims it is his and wishes to build an airship port there. The Shah has an army, but no money, and cannot afford to upset the Governors. The Governor has money from collecting tax, but no army, and cannot afford to upset the Shah.

"The Army here isn't paid, although money is sent to it. It collects from the villages and city. The Governor pays for protection, buying equipment for villagers to defend themselves. The troops here just take what they want, and the army listens to no-one."

"What would they do when we use the place for our base?" Lieutenant Hawkins asked abruptly.

Thomas winced at Lieutenant Hawkins' less than diplomatic tone. He thought he saw a smile flicker across the girl's face.

The Imam put his hands together around his cup. "The Shah would order the Army to remove you. The Army would refuse to do so. He would then tell you to stop the Governor from using it. He would tell everyone he gave you permission. The Governor would permit you to stay, for fair payment to him personally. The Army would ignore you, because you can fight back."

"What about other problems?" Thomas asked.

"It was a burial place for the old religion. Bodies laid out for the weather and animals. There are unwise farmers who think that spirits walk there when the moon is weak."

"Superstitious mumbo-jumbo," said Lieutenant Hawkins.

Thomas spoke quickly. "Would the local people object if we stirred up the superstitious mumbo-jumbo?"

"You will need an Imam to give his agreement. Bless, I think, is your word."

"Would local people help build it?"

"If they were fairly paid."

"What about the Army Brigade. What's going on with that? Who's in charge?"

"It is a Royal Prince, Firuz Yazdi. A young man with worldly ambitions."

The girl poured more tea for Thomas, her eyes averted from him. As he took the cup, their fingers touched.

"A Royal Prince commanding a brigade?" queried Lieutenant Hawkins.

The Imam frowned and sighed with disapproval. "When Shah Qajar travels, he often leaves behind Royal Princes with his host's wives and daughters. There are said to be several hundred Royal Princes around the country. He is proud to boast that only fathers sons, never daughters."

Thomas couldn't help himself. "But the odds of that ..."

"If he fathers a son, he acknowledges it, pays the mother for the upkeep, and finds him a position when the Royal Prince is of age." The Imam sounded angry, although he was trying to keep it under control. "Since he does not father daughters, he does not acknowledge any girls born. They do not officially exist. The fate of the mother and child varies. Officially, my niece here does not exist, but she is an honourable girl. Although she does have flights of fancy from her writings." The affection was evident in his voice.

"This Royal Prince. What's he like?"

"He is young. He is modern. He is fond of physical pleasure, and he is easily swayed by those who say what he wishes to hear. If you will forgive me, he will not talk with a lowly Lieutenant. Status is important for a Royal Prince."

"One more thing," Lieutenant Hawkins asked. "Why do you want us to stay in this city?"

The Imam looked surprised at the question. "Because when you are here, the bazaar is safe."

Lieutenant Hawkins stood up, and Thomas followed suit. The girl stood up and glanced at her uncle, who was speaking with Lieutenant Hawkins. She stepped close to Thomas.

"Please excuse. I wrote a flight of fancy. Perhaps you would be amused to read it." She pressed a notepad into his hand before going to stand next to her uncle. Thomas noticed that she walked very gracefully, like a dancer.

*****

"Two section patrols, setting out from here and scouting the terrain around the planned base. Getting to know the area. Two patrols, two sections to each patrol. Make nice to the locals. When the Regiment arrives, we'll be their guides for some time. One section will stay here. Rotating through. The patrols are to find things out, they're not fighting patrols."

"Two section patrols, Sir?" asked Sergeant Taylor.

"If the Persian Army gets frisky, a one section patrol might not be big enough. Sergeant Taylor, you'll take Sections 1 and 2. Cover to the north and west of the site. Lieutenant Campbell, Sections 3 and 4. Cover to the south and east. Where villages are, roads, difficult terrain, the usual. Don't get into a fight. If one comes to you, your priority is to get back intact. I expect you back in eight hours. Corporal Barry. The blacks need rifle training."

*****

"Peter, there's no point telling these people about the power of the proletariat. They don't speak English and you don't speak Persian. They think you're mad."

"Windy, in a properly organised socialist state, everyone would speak English."

"Yes, well, until they do, you've got a problem. Unless you learn to speak Persian."

"Windy, how can I learn Persian? Have you seen their writing? It's written backwards and it doesn't have letters."

*****

There are various ways of scouting, Thomas mused. One piece of intelligence that they needed was to find out who had been bribing the Persian forces. That and what they were being bribed to do. And getting a feel for what their camp was like when you could see it properly.

He thought about dressing up as a Persian and just going into the camp. It was a bit risky, but it would enable him to get a close look at things.

He thought about it a bit more. Maybe trying to disguise himself as a Persian to infiltrate a Persian camp wasn't going to be that easy. He didn't speak the language *that* fluently.

He thought about it a bit more. Maybe it was a bad idea. There was a lot about Persian life he didn't understand. It probably wasn't worth the risk.

Besides, he was thinking about this wrong. They wanted to find out who the Europeans were. They had been in a car. The car would have to use a road. It didn't come to the city, so it must have gone away from the city. Cars were rare enough out here that villagers would have seen it, and probably noticed, and maybe could describe the uniforms of the people inside the car.

All he needed was a horse, some Persian clothing, and some bits that he could pretend to be selling.

*****

"Sir, Lieutenant Campbell isn't here, but he's supposed to be acquiring mules for the base and the screw-guns. I know horses, I can tell good from bad, and Hayastan can speak the language. Perhaps I should start looking for suppliers."

"Looking, not buying, O'Grady. Until we get settled in, we've no way of keeping them."

"That's what I thought, Sir. Maybe I could rent one. Try it out for the day, see whether it's up to standard, return it to the owner."

"What are you scheming, O'Grady?"

"Truthfully, Sir? Mule racing. If I have inside information about the mules, I can clean up."

*****

No-one would suspect a man travelling along a road with a child. They'd suspect even less a man, woman, and child together. He only knew one woman in the city, the Imam's niece. Perhaps he could ask her. He wondered whether it would be advisable to ask the Imam first.

He seemed well-disposed to them. On the other hand, he'd probably say no. He'd probably assume Thomas had dishonourable intentions.

*****

"Hayastan, would you like a trip on a mule out of the city? With a Princess?" He explained his plan.

"You're marrying a Princess!" she said excitedly.

"We'll just be going for a ride."

"No. If she is alone with you, you must either be a relative or married. That's the rule." Hayastan was very firm on this.

"I can't marry her. I've already got a lady."

"Well, silly, she would be your second wife. What's her name?"

That was a point. "I'm not sure. But I can't have two wives. Not that I've got one. Well, I want to, but it's complicated."

"Why can't you have two wives? You're supposed to have three. It's the rule."

"That's not how we do things in England."

"Silly. We're not in England. We're here, so you need three wives. What's the name of your first wife?"

"Emily, but she's not my first wife. My only wife."

"Emaleh. That means the moon. She is your first wife and Princess is your second, but you need a third. What colour hair does Emaleh and Princess have?"

"Emily's got red hair and Princess has black hair and why am I even talking about this?"

"That means your third wife must have hair the colour of the sun. I'll look for one for you."

*****

Sanity prevailed. He decided asking the Princess might lead to complications.

"Sir, I thought I'd take the mule for a little trip out of the city. See how it copes with the roads." He had also decided not telling Lieutenant Hawkins would be a mistake. He didn't want to get accused of desertion. Not again.

"O'Grady, you've got some devious scheme brewing. I want the truth. What is it about?"

Time to come clean, Thomas thought. He explained. Lieutenant Hawkins considered the idea.

"How are you going to explain the fact that the girl will be doing the talking?"

"Bandage round my jaw. Broken jaw. Can't talk, Sir."

"If only," Lieutenant Hawkins muttered. He considered the idea further. "You'll be on your own."

"Yes, Sir. One, four, nine, doesn't make much difference. Someone on the road might have seen something. If we know who those Europeans were, we might be able to work out what their scheme is, and that'll make it easier to stop."

*****

After all that, no-one paid the least attention to a father and daughter walking along the road. Hayastan enjoyed riding on the mule. Once they passed the Persian Army base, they stopped at houses and asked about the car that passed.

Some of them looked arrogantly at him, and called him Armenian with a sneer, but he was a lot bigger than most of them, so they didn't say it too loudly. He repeated the questions about the car, but no-one seemed to have paid it much attention.

One farmer scowled and gave Thomas an answer. "They were crooks, though. Bought some cheese and slipped in a bad coin with the others."

Thomas asked to see the coin. "Can I buy this coin from you?" After some haggling, he bought in for 4 *shahi*. He had no idea what a 10-*pfennig* coin was worth in Persian money, but the farmer was glad of the exchange.

"Who is prettier, Emaleh or the Princess?"

It was going to be a long journey back to the city. Let her chatter, and she'll have forgotten everything by the time they got back. Children never remembered anything.

*****

Patrolling without packs was a relief. They would be returning and Hayastan was safe with the packs back in the city, along with Section 1.

Lieutenant Hawkins had made it clear that they were on a reconnaissance patrol, not a fighting patrol and that they would be patrolling in parallel with Section 3. Close enough to support each other, far enough away that they could cover more ground. That involved constantly sending runners between the sections whenever they were out of sight of each other, but luckily, the Zulus never seemed to get tired of running.

Frank had decided to cover the ground between the planned base and the Persian camp. The other patrol was covering the ground between the planned base and the city. Lieutenant Hawkins had emphasised that the primary purpose of these patrol was to get everyone familiar with the terrain. He'd repeated himself several times.

Thomas wondered what was going on. Germans paying the Persian Army commander when the Regiment was due to arrive didn't make much sense. With the Regiment on the spot, whatever the Persian Army did, the Regiment would be able to quickly put a stop to it. Whatever was being planned, they would do better if the Regiment was nowhere near the scene when it started.

"Mind on job, O'Grady," Frank snapped.

They walked on. The city quickly gave way to farmland. To start with, the farmers ignored the Riflemen as they walked past.

Everything seemed to be normal. The fields varied in size and shape and seemed to have boundaries that were determined to be anything other than straight.

As they got further away from the city, something didn't feel quite right. Thomas wasn't quite sure what it was, but it wasn't right. It was like harvest time back on the estate, but different, and he didn't think it was just a different way of doing things.

The farmers looked scared and sullen and not at all happy to see the patrol. They worked in the middle of the fields, so it was hard to tell much about their expressions.

That was the odd thing. They were harvesting in the middle of the field, but they'd left the edges alone. They were having difficulty getting the crop they were harvesting out of the field and into the carts. There were a number of carts being filled and, one by one, they headed off eastwards, which was odd. The nearest village was to the west, but there weren't any villages close at hand in the direction the carts were going.

He pointed this out to Frank. "We need to know what's on those carts and where they're going."

"I am Corporal. You are Rifleman. I give orders. You right, but stop taking command. It's not good on patrol."

The difficulty was following the carts while staying out of sight. They managed it, with Frank's section covering an arc behind and to the left, while the other section covered the other side. Thomas was almost directly behind the cart.

The track over which the cart was travelling was rutted and hard, so Thomas kept a close eye on the ground. Sure enough, the cart jolted heavily over a hole, and he saw some of the produce falling off the cart. He kept an eye on where it had fallen and picked up some of it when he passed it.

Flowers? They were harvesting flowers?

The line of the patrol came slowly to a halt as those at the front saw something and went to ground, copied by the next in line.

Slowly, they worked their way together, and Thomas found they'd reached a wood.

"Persian base other side of this wood," Frank said in a whisper. "Davie, Thomas, go very carefully, see if anything to be seen. Stay hidden priority. Not take chances."

Thomas wondered why Frank had chosen the two biggest men in the section to scout ahead, when they needed to stay unseen. The trees were densely packed, with little undergrowth. Any noise they might have made was swamped by the noise of the cart trundling along the track.

The cart came to a gate in the fence surrounding the base and half a dozen guards swarmed around the cart, inspecting it. Then they took it from the farmer, who waited.

"We need to see inside the base," Thomas whispered to Davie. Davie pointed to a tree. The branches lower than head high had been cut off, presumably removed by the Persian soldiers for use as firewood, but above this, the branches were thick and numerous. Davie formed a stirrup with his hands and gave Thomas a platform to enable him to pull himself up onto the first branch.

Once he had got onto the first branch, it was just a matter of remembering his childhood and scrambling upwards until he got a clear view.

He was just in time to see the cart being dragged through to the centre of the camp and brought to a halt beside a lorry. Soldiers started transferring the load from the cart into the lorry. This didn't take long, then they dragged the cart back towards the gate, while the flaps were pulled down on the lorry, which then drove off.

Thomas clambered down the tree, and he and Davie reported back to Frank. Frank considered the information.

"We cut short patrol. Lieutenant Hawkins want this information soon."

As they headed back, Thomas considered the flowers he had picked up. He didn't like to admit it, but that doctor might be able to tell him what they were. He just didn't like the doctor.

*****

"You really don't know what this is?" Doctor Hashemi looked surprised as he held the flower, looking at it with some distaste.

"I'm just an ignorant rifleman. I'm a city boy."

"An ignorant rifleman who has learned enough Persian to talk with us? I shudder to think how knowledgeable graduates from Oxford must be."

Thomas waited, sipping tea in the doctor's house, an airy place, with a very high roof. In England, it would have been possible to have two rooms, one above the other. "Talking's easy. Knowing things is harder. Would you be a married man, Sir?" He tried to sound casual as he asked the question.

"Alas, I have spent so long studying to be a doctor. Being a doctor takes up so much time that I have not yet married. I rather think I am married to medicine. The numbers are not in my favour."

Thomas frowned. "I thought Muslim men could marry three wives."

"And there is the problem. The rich and powerful take their pick. Some, like the Shah, take more than their allotted three. The farmers and the labourers arrange things within their own village. Those like myself, in the middle, are kept busy with our work, and when we look, the cupboard is bare. In the meantime, I treat the sick."

Thomas felt his heart sink. A nurse would have so much in common with a doctor than with him. "The flower. What is it?"

"An opium poppy, of course. I use them to make painkillers. I would be grateful for what you have. That would be a week's supply for me. In quantities above a few plants, it will be to make opium or heroin."

Thomas thanked him for his time, then stepped outside, feeling miserable. He needed to throw himself into his work. The trouble was, as a rifleman, he didn't have much to think about. Frank was busy. He was effectively a senior NCO, and he had a great deal to do.

Thomas felt like getting drunk and even that seemed like it was going to be difficult.

*****

Windy and Peter found a park with a pool in it. The pool had a pavilion at one end, with columns from the pavilion reflected in the water. There were paintings on the walls of the pavilion. An air of peace hung over the place.

"You're not as annoyed as you sometimes are," Windy said.

"There's a lot in the world to make anyone angry."

"Try and change the world, and you'll get nowhere. Change it a little bit at a time."

"That'll take forever," Peter said. "Sometimes it just seems too much. Too much for one person."

"What are buddies for?"

"You're just in here to make money for your family. Nothing wrong with that, it's got to be done."

"Maybe when my family's settled, I'll want to try and make sure no-one else has no choice. We're buddies, OK?"

*****

"In a land far away, a nobleman lived in a house that was a palace." Thomas read from the story the Imam's niece had given him. Hayastan had asked him to tell her a story and he wasn't very good at coming up with stories of his own. She was lying down, head rested against Davie, who was listening as he cleaned his equipment.

"The nobleman was rich and had everything he needed. He was content. He had a son. The son was tall and handsome and charming and healthy. He had everything he could desire, but he was not happy. He didn't have to work, and he had everything he wanted. He looked across his father's lands and he saw people who worked hard, and who had nothing, and this made him sad.

"So, the son packed his bags, took on a new name, and went to seek adventure in a place where no-one knew who he was. He met many people, and he made good friends, and they had many adventures.

"Together with his friends, they travelled to this land. When they arrived, this land was troubled with bad men who were powerful. Magicians who took everything from people and who did not hold the Prophet in honour. People who worked for the bad men did not obey the law and were very cruel.

"They arrived in the city where Abla lived. Abla was a young woman, and she hated the cruelty of the bad man, but what could one young woman do? She had tried, but no-one listened to a young woman.

"Then the son saw Abla, and Abla saw him, and they drank tea together, and as they drank, their fingers touched. When that happened, she fell in love with him, and he fell in love with her. They talked, and they walked beneath the all-knowing moon, and they counted the columns in the pool of love, and they knew perfect joy.

"In the morning, they swore that they would be together for all time and that together they would rid the land of evil. And this was the start of their adventures together."

Hayastan was asleep, curled up against Davie. Davie smiled ruefully. "You know you're going to have to read the next episode to us tomorrow. I want to find out what happens to them."

Thomas wondered if he ought to explain things to Abla.

*****

"O'Grady, stop wool-gathering," said Lieutenant Hawkins. "I need your devious mind. What's going on with these shipments?"

Thomas stood up, while Hayastan continued to sleep curled up against Davie. "Yes, Sir. Could be many things, Sir."

"Such as?"

Thomas gathered his thoughts. Maybe if he said nothing to Abla, the whole thing would blow over. Whatever the whole thing was. On the other hand, if he said nothing, maybe she'd imagine things and say something to her uncle, and that could lead to complications. On the other hand, if he did say something, she might misinterpret and then things could get complicated. On the other hand, if she misunderstood, then he'd see and he could put her right. On the other hand, didn't Hayastan say something about not being alone with a woman unless one was a relative or married? If he tried to explain, that might cause complications. On the other hand, if he explained when her uncle was there, he might get the wrong impression and that could lead to big complications. It was complicated.

"In your own time, O'Grady."

"Yes, Sir," said Thomas, feeling like a confused octopus. "Germans give money to the Prince. The Prince gives opium to the Germans. They're taking it somewhere, probably selling it on and making a fortune. The Prince doesn't pay his troops, so he's collecting money from the Germans, from the Persian King, *and* from taxing the locals. Either he's greedy, or he needs the money for something big. Whatever that is, he doesn't need his own troops for it, because they're not happy and won't fight for him. The Persian troops might be loyal to the King, but if they've all deserted and become bandits, then he can use the money to hire foreign troops who will be loyal to him and not the King. The Germans won't want just a little disturbance that's easily put down, especially now we're here, so they'll be keen to make sure that any disturbance is a big one. Sir."

"Thank you, O'Grady. Your devious mind is always reliable."

*****

Thomas had to explain the situation to Abla. If he allowed it to go, things could get out of hand. He had to control the situation, not allow the situation to control him. Unchecked, things could get out of hand.

He knocked at the door. Abla answered, looking down at the ground. "My uncle is not in, I'm afraid. He'll be back in the morning."

"Actually, it was you I wanted to talk to, Abla."

"Abla? You've read my story? When my uncle returns, you could tell me what you think." She paused, and then looked up at Thomas, brown eyes wide and her voice slightly shaking. "Or you could come in for tea and tell me what you think now."

*****

The Imam read through a couple of letters that had arrived. News from other Imams. There was much to consider. Rather than travel to the meeting place, he would return home to contemplate the implications of this news.

*****

"If she is alone with you, you must either be a relative or married. That's the rule." That's what Hayastan had said. He looked at Abla, at her wide, hopeful eyes. He knew that if he went inside, he would give way to temptation.

Would that be so bad? Abla was pretty, and willing, and it wasn't as though he had any commitments.

"Be careful, Thomas." That was the last thing Emily had said to him before he'd set off. Maybe there was still hope there. There wouldn't be if he went inside.

"Abla, if I come inside, that would lead to dishonour, and I will only treat with you honourably."

"You would consider my honour, although I am but a woman who does not exist? You are the one I have dreamt about."

"Abla, there is already someone in my heart."

"And I would be proud to be your second wife."

"I shall come back when your uncle returns."

"I shall wait. I shall try to be worthy of you. If you wish to wait for his return inside?"

"That would be wrong, and I shall not bring wrong upon you." He turned and returned to the Section.

The trouble was, he'd never be able to tell Emily how he had avoided temptation. And all because he held a faint hope that all was not lost. He wondered if he had made a mistake by not taking advantage of the situation.

*****

Frank missed Joy. He missed seeing her smile when he called on her in the morning. He missed her touch on his arm when they walked together.

He loved her. He didn't understand why she loved him, but she did. This worried him. He didn't deserve her and there would be a payment. She'd told him not to be silly, but he still worried.

She wanted to marry him. He wanted to marry her, but he wanted it to be a proper marriage. There was a problem. The more time he spent with her, the more he wanted to be with her, but he didn't want to dishonour her by sleeping with her before marriage.

He was so very lucky. The trouble was, good fortune always had to be paid for, and he was scared at what the price was going to be.

*****

Lieutenant Hawkins paced around the bazaar, making sure that he was out of sight of the men. He knew he was getting out of his depth. It was ironic, in a way. He'd developed this scheme for small-scale units operating under their own initiative.

He'd seen how hard this was to deal with. It was like trying to grab smoke. He'd decided that to deal with this sort of smoke, you had to fight fire with fire, that such units would be very disruptive of a regular army opposition. He'd been able to gather, train, and encourage a likely-looking group with a wide-range of skills, and they were shaping up better than anyone could have imagined.

However, when it came to putting theory into practise in the field, the men were performing well, and he was the one who was too set in his ways to handle the new way of doing things. These last few days had seen him fall short of the standard the platoon should expect from him.

There was just so much diplomacy and lateral thinking required. He was struggling.

"You have news, Sergeant Taylor?"

Sergeant Taylor nodded. "Yes, Sir. Got word that the Regional Governor has got wind of things and has decided to pay a visit. He'll apparently want to speak with you tomorrow when he gets here."

"What does he want to talk about?"

"Word is that he wants to talk about our future base. Specifically, airship landing facilities."

"Anything else?"

"Yes, Sir. More bad news. He'll be bringing along an archaeologist. Finding old junk for his university."

"Not that maniac Evans?"

"No, Sir."

"Thank God for that."

"I'm afraid it's worse, Sir. It's an American, working for the University of Chicago. Professor Mark Hertzberg. Apparently, he's eccentric."

"How eccentric?"

"As eccentric as a hatter, I understand, Sir."

"Shouldn't that be mad as a hatter?"

"He's rich, Sir. Therefore, he's eccentric. I'm afraid there's more, Sir. The Governor is bringing along a token of his esteem. To help us see things his way with regard to the base, Sir."

"Just how bad is it?"

"He wants one of his sons to join the Regiment."

"Go on. Why is this a major problem? We're taking Persian recruits."

"He's twelve. Word is the Governor believes Major to be the right rank for one of his sons."

"No. Over my dead body."

"You might need to find a more diplomatic way of phrasing that, Sir. Who knows, maybe we'll be able to form a regiment of children yet, Sir. Hayastan, now this young gentleman."

"When I say over my dead body, Sergeant, I mean that if you make any more suggestions like that, it'll be over your dead body."

*****

When the Imam returned to his home, he noticed that his niece seemed flustered. He asked her why and was suspicious when she evaded answering.

"Answer truly," he said.

"The Rifleman came to speak with me. I told him that you were not here, and he said he would return when you had returned. He said that it was not right for him to be with me without your being present. He is an honourable man."

The Imam corrected her. "He behaved in an honourable manner. Whether that makes him an honourable man is another matter."

"He cares for the wounded. He protects the weak. He looks after the orphans. How much more does he need to do to prove his worth?"

"For you? I think I shall be convinced when he has laid down his life for you. Hush, I shall speak with him tomorrow."

*****

This was going to test his ability to speak Persian. He needed to find a tailor in the bazaar, then explain his requirements. He wanted a uniform in rifleman green but sized for a seven-year-old girl. A mascot had to look the part.

Throwing himself into doing things and keeping busy helped stop him thinking about Emily. And Abla.

*****

Davie showed Hayastan how to hold the two sticks. "With this one, you attack. With the other one, you defend. This is how we play Lintonga."

Charlie and Davie demonstrated. One by one, other members of the platoon came to watch.

"When does it end?" Rifleman Callaghan asked.

"When one person gives up, surrenders," Billie explained.

"I don't think it's a girl's game," Rifleman Callaghan said.

"It's a warrior's game."

*****

"I hear that you called last night, Rifleman."

"Yes, Sir. But you were not here."

"Was it me you called to speak to?"

Thomas paused, uncertain how to answer. The trouble was, he didn't know how much the Imam knew and how much he guessed. The thing to do in such circumstances was not to lie, but to give away as little information as possible while trying to work out how much he did know. "I wished to speak with your niece, but you were not here."

"Wouldn't that have allowed less hindered conversation?"

"It would have been improper and would have offended your customs." Thomas paused. "With respect, Sir, you seem to know a lot about our rank structure."

"I knew this regiment would be coming. You came to speak with my niece?"

"I wished to thank her for the story she gave me to read. Hayastan, the orphan child, enjoyed it very much."

"I shall write another for her, if you will permit, uncle."

"It is a flight of fancy, and not productive."

"With respect, sir, it gave pleasure to a young girl. The pleasure of that young girl gave pleasure to myself and one of my comrades."

The Imam looked long and hard at Thomas. "I will consider your words. You may return in the evening to collect the next flight of fancy."

*****

Thomas was worried. He was worried about a lot of things. About Emily, about Hayastan, about Abla, about how complicated this whole situation was, about the Persian recruits they'd be getting. But, most of all, he was worrying about how much the Imam seemed to know about them.

The stuff that he knew, what a person's rank was without being told, what the relative level of the ranks were, all sorts of little things. Mostly what was troubling him was how quickly the Imam seemed to be accepting Thomas seeing Abla. Abla was a Princess, in effect, and he was just a foreign soldier, not even an officer.

Come to that, the story Abla wrote was just too perfectly aimed at him. This whole thing about being the man of her dreams, well, far-fetched didn't even start to cover that.

And the Imam seemed to keep popping up for discussions. *And* he seemed only too happy to explain things, in what was a complicated situation. Was that business about Abla being a Royal Princess even true? He'd never heard about a King happily acknowledging bastards if they were male, and not girl bastards.

It was easy to get paranoid, but what was the angle here? Come to that, where was the rest of Abla's family? Her mother, any others. Living alone with her uncle, that was just too convenient.

Assume the Imam was more than he seemed. Was Abla even his niece? There was no family resemblance, although that didn't prove much. If there had been, it would have, but no resemblance didn't mean no connection.

The situation was complicated. The King, the Governor, the Royal Prince and the Army here, the Imam, the villagers and the bandits, the Germans, and possibly others he didn't know about, and they all seemed to have their own agenda. Then there was the situation with Emily, Abla, the doctor, Hayastan, Frank and Joy, and probably others that he didn't know about.

How on earth was he going to disentangle things? Maybe he should desert and join the French Foreign Legion. That would be a goodwill gesture.

*****

"Windy, I've been thinking."

"Well, that's your problem right there," Windy said to Peter.

"No, seriously. The thing is, we always knew that these Persian recruits are going to be bad."

"Not much we can do about that, Peter."

"Well, there is. Look at them working in the market. Some of them are likely looking lads."

"Maybe. Nothing we can do about it."

"That's just it. There is. We just need to persuade these guys to volunteer, fill up the slots, then we can tell the rubbish from the Persian Army to take a hike."

Windy understood how Peter thought. "I see. And you reckon that while these guys are with us, you'd be able to teach them Socialisationing. Then, when we go home, you'll be releasing into this city fifty, maybe a hundred trained soldiers, all in one place, all eager to overthrow the corrupt, elitist regime and replace it with a worker's paradise. Maybe repeat it in other cities we goes to."

"It's not a bad plan. We get decent soldiers, and Persia gets a properly-run society."

"There's just one problem, Peter. You don't speak Persian."

*****

"Just one Section, Sir?" Sergeant Taylor was concerned. "I know we're not expecting trouble at the station, but why should we send anyone?"

"Because, like it or not, the Governor is powerful. I want to be on hand when he arrives and get a good look at him first thing. It's a mark of respect and it might earn us a bit of credit. What's more, it shows the Persians that we're here and looking after things."

"Yes, Sir. What about the Persian Army?"

"That's another reason. If they're going to do anything against the Governor, they'll do it at the station. Once the Governor's inside the city proper, those involved will get caught. At the station, they would be able to make a getaway if we aren't there."

"Just one Section, Sir?"

"I want the others out of sight. That way, if retribution needs to be taken, we've the forces on hand that can do it."

*****

Two miles out of the city and waiting on the platform for the train to arrive. Full kit. Rifles not loaded, but everyone in the section had as many spare magazines as they could acquire. Hayastan stood at the end of the line next to Thomas, trying unsuccessfully not to beam with smiles in her new Rifleman uniform.

Frank gave orders to the Section. Abe repeated these orders to the Zulus, mimicking Frank's gestures, and Hayastan repeated the orders to Thomas, Peter, and Windy, copying Abe's gestures. The tailor had included corporal's stripes on Hayastan's uniform, and Thomas had explained to her that this was because she was the Corporal of the Mascots.

Several officers from the Persian Army were there, including the Royal Prince, resplendent in the uniform festooned with medals. Since he was in his early twenties, it seemed unlikely that they were hard-earned awards. He was somewhat non-descript in appearance and he appeared to have a somewhat distracted and vacant air about him. He ignored the Section entirely, apart from a single comment. It wasn't clear who, if anyone, he was addressing, but he described the Section as "scruffy."

The Imam was there as well, along with a man of a similar age to him.

"Who's that with the Mayor?" Lieutenant Hawkins asked Thomas.

"That will be the Imam, Sir. That's the one you keep calling the Mayor. The Mayor is the other one."

"How do you know this, O'Grady." He glanced across to where Abla was standing just behind her uncle. He sighed. "Never mind,

I see how. Put you in a monastery and you'd still find a way to get into trouble with women."

"Is that her?" Hayastan whispered in a voice that echoed around the station. "She's very pretty. She'll be a good second wife for you."

"How dead do you think he'll be when Nurse Charrington arrives with the Regiment?" Windy wondered aloud.

"You're a fine one to talk. Beryl and Iris, with not a thought of sharing."

"Well, they're in London and we aren't, so that's not a problem anymore."

"Unless they come out here to entertain the troops," Peter said.

"Silence in the ranks," said Frank.

"Silence in the ranks," said Abe.

"Silence in the ranks," squeaked Hayastan.

"Just the once," said Lieutenant Hawkins. "No need for multiple orders. O'Grady, front and centre." This was getting problematic, he knew, having O'Grady along all the time, but the man seemed to understand how these people thought. "What do you make of the Prince?"

"Hard to say, Sir. Especially when there are people around us who can speak English."

"Good point, O'Grady."

A train approached and Frank called the men to attention. Lieutenant Hawkins focussed on the matter in hand. When things get complicated, focus on one thing, deal with it. You unravel a twisted knot one string at a time. The trick was to work out which was the most important string. The Royal Prince controlled the Persian Army, so he was the one with the firepower on hand. That made him the most urgent problem. Agreements about the base, that was something that Colonel Dalkeith would need to finalise.

As far as Lieutenant Hawkins could tell, the Prince seemed to be disinterested, pre-occupied. The train came to a stop, then dozens of doors on the carriage opened and a flood of people emerged. Men, women, young, old.

A middle-aged man, maybe fifty years old, seemed to be the centre of attention. Overweight and moving slowly, but with a genial smile. Young man next to him, and a boy on the other side. Next to the boy was an athletic-looking man of much the same age as the Governor, with grey hair and a European look. Half a dozen impeccably dressed soldiers and a similar number of young women, following behind the Governor.

The Governor walked slowly and everyone in his entourage walked at his pace. The Royal Prince walked towards them and they greeted each other with all the warmth of enemies who were pretending to be friends. Then the Prince spoke briefly with the archaeologist, simply saying that he would be at his camp and looked forward to speaking with him there. Then he turned and left, the other officers following, ignoring Lieutenant Hawkins entirely.

"You understand these people, O'Grady. What's the protocol?"

"They're the ones with the position and influence. You're the one with the guns. The city needs you, especially now that the Royal Prince has graced us with his absence. You just need to be the rock about which they try and manoeuvre."

The Governor came across and spoke with the Mayor and the Imam, and then he looked at Abla.

"Your daughter?" he asked the Mayor.

"My niece," said the Imam. Abla looked concerned.

"Pleasing. Have her delivered to my rooms."

"I'm afraid not, Sir," O'Grady said.

"And why not, Sir?" asked the Governor, an amused tone to his voice.

"Protection of the British Army, Sir."

"I see. It's a bold private who questions a Governor. Would you have a personal interest?"

"Rifleman, Sir, not Private." Thomas frowned. That came across badly, as he had to use the same word for both terms.

"Interesting. And one who speaks our language. Not well, I grant you, but well enough. Commendable."

Thomas felt uncomfortable with everyone's attention being on him. "If you say so, Sir."

"And the girl is yours?"

"With respect, Sir, she is under the protection of the British Army."

"I shall give you two of my wives for her. Two for one, and you may choose the two. That's a good deal, for both of us."

"Protection of the British Army doesn't work like that, Sir."

"When you are older, you value variety more than you do when in the first flush of youth. Two wives and a horse? No? Well, may she give you the pleasure you deserve." The Governor chuckled. "And, young man, you've shown me that the British will stick by an agreement, which pleases me. We shall discuss business in a cooler place."

As he led the way towards the vehicles to take them into the city, several people seemed to want to speak with Thomas.

"You never said you could speak Persian, O'Grady."

"You never asked, Sir."

"I'll deal with you later, O'Grady."

The Imam stood in front of Thomas. The crowd were still sorting themselves out. One of the Governor's wives gave Thomas a very long look.

"You named yourself the protector of my niece?"

"Protection of the British Army, Sir."

"No, Rifleman O'Grady. It was not the British Army that stood and said no to a Governor to protect my niece from dishonour. Humility is a virtue, but false humility is not humility at all. I shall consider further what this means. I trust you with her protection."

Abla spoke briefly to Thomas, before following her uncle. "You are the man of my dreams."

Thomas sighed. Try as he might, things were getting very complicated.

*****

It was inevitable, Thomas thought. They had come to a well-appointed house just outside the bazaar in order to discuss a number of matters with the Governor. There was a lot to discuss. While they were served tea, the archaeologist dominated the conversation.

It was not so much a conversation as a monologue. He was an American, Professor Mark Herzberg of the University of Chicago, and he had come to seek out antiquities and acquire them for the University, and he was prepared to pay top dollar for the best. He planned to go to Persepolis, and he had a great theory. According to him, there had long been a tradition of annual gifts being given from the Persian nobility to the King here, where it was stored. This was hidden when Alexander approached, and the location of the hiding place lost. Until now. He, Professor Mark Herzberg, had unlocked the secret, and when located these lost treasures, he would become the greatest and most famous archaeologist since Schliemann. "*He* only gazed on the face of Agamemnon. *I* will gaze upon the face of Alexander."

Thomas couldn't help himself. He knew he should just keep his mouth shut. He knew he should. "Excuse me, Professor. If the treasures were hidden because Alexander was approaching, and if he never found them, then why would there be a face mask of him there? Surely the Persians wouldn't have made a face mask of the person who was busy killing them and destroying their city? I don't see how they would have had the time."

"There will be bandits and dangers, but archaeology is not for the faint-hearted. It needs a pioneering, adventurous spirit. But I have reason to believe that there is a treasure there of even greater value than priceless artefacts. I cannot breathe a word of this theory of mine, but it will make the discovery of Noah's Ark on Mount Ararat pale into insignificance. I can say no more."

"Thank God," murmured Thomas.

"I will only say that when the Babylonians enslaved the Israelites, they also took with them the greatest treasure of the Israelites, and this I shall recover."

"Good luck with that," said Lieutenant Hawkins.

"And I will need to hire local labourers and European guards. Major Hawkins, I will pay you handsomely to organise this."

"My orders do not permit me to do so. Good luck," Lieutenant Hawkins replied abruptly.

"Try the Persian troops," Thomas suggested. They know the area They will work well for people who pay them."

Lieutenant Hawkins nodded. If it got some of the Persian troops 400 miles away, that would be one less problem.

"I shall go and speak to them." He left, and the room breathed a sigh of relief. That allowed the Governor to discuss matters with Lieutenant Hawkins through Thomas.

"The Governor's name is Akbar Massoud. He has been Governor here since he was thirteen. He has twelve wives, sixteen sons, and twenty-three daughters."

"Tell the Governor I am John Hawkins. I have been in the Army since I was thirteen. I have no wives, no sons, and no daughters."

"He says his heart is heavy at your misfortune in life. He will find a wife for you, as a mark of the goodwill he wishes between us."

"That won't be necessary."

The Governor spoke for a long time in reply.

"He said, oh." Thomas paused.

"Tell me exactly what he said, O'Grady. I can't answer if I don't know just what was said."

"Yes, Sir. He said that I had acquired a taste for ladies of Persia."

"What else did he say?" Lieutenant Hawkins could tell that Thomas had summarised quite extensively.

"It's difficult to translate, Sir."

"Try."

"Some of the terms and customs, they're, well, I'm not familiar with them, Sir."

"Stop beating about the bush, O'Grady."

"Yes, Sir. The young ladies are gifts to the British officers, as a mark of his welcoming the Regiment to the region."

"Carry on, O'Grady."

"Yes, Sir. Sir, I would suggest you don't respond angrily. He said I could have first pick for a wife if I persuaded you to take one of these young ladies to be your wife. The lady would be greatly honoured."

"Tell him no."

"Sir, they would be his eyes into our base. They would send reports back to him and he would see that we're operating honestly. He would learn all that they get to see, Sir, and we would know who was doing the looking." Thomas hoped that Lieutenant Hawkins picked up on the implication. "I thought not as wives, but we were thinking of hiring servants for the officers, Sir."

"The answer's still no."

Thomas translated.

Lieutenant Hawkins frowned. "That took a long time to say no, O'Grady. What did you say?"

"A Persian no, Sir. I thanked him for his kind and gracious and generous offer, that you expressed your warmest feelings towards the offer, and that you would give your strongest recommendation to Colonel Dalkeith when he arrives, for such a decision would be the Colonel's to make."

"Has anyone ever told you that you're very devious, O'Grady?"

"People seem to say nothing else, Sir."

Negotiations can't be hurried, so they drank tea and considered the fine quality of the rugs. Then the Governor raised the subject of his son joining the Regiment to learn while the Regiment was here. The boy was brought forward. Maybe twelve years old, slightly tending towards pudginess, serious expression, polite.

"What's your name?" Thomas asked.

The boy glanced towards the Governor.

"No," snapped Thomas. "If you're to be a soldier, you will be a soldier. Your father won't be out in the field. When an officer like Lieutenant Hawkins asks a soldier a question, they answer. Clearly, accurately, without deception. What is your name?"

"Esmail Mirza Motamed ed-Dowleh," the boy said, standing straight.

"That's a bit of a mouthful. Esmail Dowling is probably as good as we'll manage. Why do you want to be a soldier in the Regiment?"

"Because my father said so."

"That's what your father wants. Why do you want to join?"

"To learn to be a man, not just a son of my father."

Thomas nodded. He understood, probably better than the boy realised. He explained to Lieutenant Hawkins.

"Find a way to say no."

"Sir, that's going to be hard. They've seen Hayastan. If he joins as a mascot, he can help out around the camp. If the work isn't to his taste, he will leave us, his fault, not ours. If we refuse to give him a fair try, the Governor will see it as our fault."

Lieutenant Hawkins had hard words about diplomacy. "Go on, then. No more than a mascot, mind. Which will mean skivvy back in camp."

"The British Army makes use of mascots."

"Is that an honourable position?" the boy asked.

"Absolutely. The British Army has the Mascot Guards, the Royal Mascot Greys, brave regiments from Mascotland.

"I have heard of Scotland, but not Mascotland."

"Same place. Mascotland is the full name." Thomas hoped Lieutenant Campbell didn't get to hear of this and rather feared he would. He noticed a twinkle in the Governor's eye at the response.

"Rifleman O'Grady," the Governor asked. "Have you ever been court martialled?"

"No, Sir." What the hell, thought Thomas. "There's an important thing about court martials. Courts martial. I always get confused over those two. There are two reasons. Firstly, I am an honourable man."

"And secondly?"

Thomas waited a moment. "And secondly, they only court martial someone if they catch them."

The Governor laughed and because he laughed, everyone else laughed. "I see we have a second Sinbad. An honest rogue. Or maybe a dishonest man of honour. Learn from this man, Esmail. He will teach you how to make your fortune and fame without my help. A mascot you shall be. Come back as a man I can be proud of."

Thomas' head was beginning to hurt. Abla gave him more tea, and her fingers brushed his hand as she did so. She smiled, her eyes sparkling, but she looked away when he glanced at her.

"The matter of your base," said the Governor. "I have a proposition. I have heard that the location you wish for your base is the location I wish to build an airship port. To my mind, this conflict of interests presents an opportunity. You will be here for two years. Build your base, with my blessing. You will want a place for your airships to land and buildings for your people to live in. When you leave, I will have the start of my port, and it will have been demonstrated to all."

"What about the King?" Lieutenant Hawkins asked when Thomas explained the proposition.

"That, I think, is the point, Sir. We get to resolve the land dispute in his favour."

"If we say no?"

"We'll need to find somewhere else, Sir. Patrols haven't found anywhere so good."

"How badly will the King take this?"

"No idea, Sir. There's one other issue, Sir. What if we don't leave?"

"We will. We're not going to be based out here forever."

"Another regiment might replace us, Sir."

"This is something for the Colonel. Explain that, O'Grady."

Thomas suspected that the Governor was well aware of every nuance of what was being said. Best face the big issue head-on. Get a reputation for being honest and open.

"What will the King think of the scheme?"

"The King has many concerns, and this is a small one among all of them. He will prefer you to have the site and keep it secure. In two years, when you leave, well, a lot can happen in two years. The King might be of a different mind. There might be another King. Much can happen. I shall remain in this city until your Colonel arrives." He glanced towards Abla. "A Rifleman who defies a Governor over the fate of a girl. You English are strange. Still, that looks like a part of Persia that you have conquered utterly."

"Protection of the British Army, Sir."

"A very specific portion of the British Army, I suspect. I also suspect that in some months, this city will have a shortage."

"A shortage, Sir? What of? Labourers?"

"Midwives, Rifleman."

*****

"You did well, O'Grady."

"Thank you, Sir."

"Why didn't you tell me you spoke Persian? No nonsense about my not asking."

"I didn't know if I was proficient, Sir. If I said I spoke it before I knew how well, it could have led to bigger problems than if I'd waited."

"I'll be advising Colonel Dalkeith. Tell Lieutenant Campbell and Sergeant Taylor I want to speak with them. Tell Corporal Barry that all patrols tomorrow are cancelled. I've got a feeling something's brewing here. This is the spot we need to be."

*****

Chaperone. All the time have a chaperone. Abla was continuing the story with Hayastan. Thomas made sure that Davie was there as well, to help settle her down to sleep.

Hayastan, not Abla. He had to avoid any temptation. The trouble was, Hayastan was right. Abla was very pretty, and she was sitting very close to him.

"Hayastan, you stay close to Rifleman Davie. I've got to check up on the officers."

"Rifleman?" asked Davie.

"Yes," said Thomas gratefully. "That's exactly it. You've fought, you've trained, you've been in the forefront of everything. I want to ask if we can call you Riflemen rather than Veteran Recruit or whatever. And I think we're going to be too busy tomorrow."

"Will you tell me a story every night? You tell very good stories."

"If Thomas allows it. He is my protector as well as yours and we must both obey him."

"That's right. I hadn't thought of that. That makes us like sisters."

Thomas left as quickly as he could. He suspected that emotional blackmail would follow soon. Being somewhere else seemed like a good idea.

"O'Grady. I want a word with you." It was Sergeant Taylor. "Hayastan, and now this Esmail? Is this a regiment of riflemen or an orphanage?"

"It will give the wives something to do when the Regiment arrives, Sergeant. It shows the locals that they don't need to be scared of us. And with Esmail, his father's Governor of the region. Be worthwhile staying on the right side of him."

"Well, until further notice, Rifleman O'Grady, you have been selected from a host of volunteers to be responsible for these children."

That didn't sound too bad.

"That means if they get into trouble, I'll be having a word with you as to how you let them."

That didn't sound so good.

"Your first job, O'Grady, is to get this latest recruit kitted out. And O'Grady, you might want to get spare kit. I've a feeling these will not be the last."

"If we get a platoon, does that mean I'll get a promotion, Sergeant?"

Each of them wondered if the other was bluffing.

*****

"That's the way to start the Revolution here," said Peter. "I've got to learn the language."

"How are you going to do that?"

"Thomas managed. It can't be that hard."

"Thomas managed because he found a pillow dictionary." Windy smiled. "You've never had much luck like that."

"That's your fault. The one time we find a couple, you go and hog them both for yourself."

"I've just had an idea," Windy said. "The Governor, he arrived with a horde of lovelies. I know where there will be a harem looking to escape. That Royal Prince will have a dozen spare pieces of tail. All we need to do is sneak in, rescue them, bask in their undying affection, and you'll get to learn all the Persian you want."

"Windy, even by your standards, that's a stupid idea."

"It worked when we stole the mess silver from the dragoons. And this mess silver will be able to walk by itself."

Peter thought about it. "Breaking into an enemy camp? That's a bit of a problem."

"They're not enemy, they're allies. They're not soldiers, they're rubbish. And we wouldn't be breaking in, we'd be breaking out."

"Windy, if your next words are going to be 'What could possibly go wrong?' I've got one word for you. Eunuchs."

*****

Thomas went to collect Esmail. The Governor was in deep discussion with the Imam and the Mayor. They had papers spread over the table. It all felt very conspiratorial to Thomas.

"Sir, I've come to collect the young man, if you're certain you want him to be with the Regiment. Hard work and we're likely to be going to places where there's some risk."

"Esmail, there might be some risk."

"Father, I have to prove myself. If there is no risk, there is no adventure. Besides, that Armenian girl was wearing a uniform. How risky can it be?"

"Permission to speak freely to your son, Sir?"

"As of this moment, he is in the Regiment. Treat him as you would any mascot." The Governor smiled indulgently, and Thomas could see him watching closely.

"That Armenian girl is Hayastan and she's already seen part of the Regiment in action. Now, the Regiment works on buddies. Everyone has a buddy and the two of you stick together. You look after each other, because that means in combat, you've got your buddy's back, and your buddy has yours. The way it works is this: during training, if you get into trouble, you get punished for getting into trouble, and your buddy gets punished for letting you get into trouble. Naturally, Hayastan is your buddy in the Regiment."

"But she's just an Armenian girl."

"She's also your buddy. That's one thing about becoming a man. You have to learn how to get on with people, even when they're from different backgrounds. You'll be surprised how much you can learn."

"But buddy with an Armenian girl?"

Thomas felt there was something he was missing here. "Sir," he said to the Governor. "My knowledge of the language is perhaps lacking. Could you explain what the confusion here is?"

"It's the word buddy that is causing him some problem. Rifleman, are buddies closer than friends?"

"I guess. You're responsible for each other. You share everything. You have each other's backs. It's like you're always together."

"And this is true for everyone in the Regiment?"

"For Riflemen, yes."

"But man and man?" the boy said.

"No, not *that*. Just close friends."

Esmail relaxed a little. "It would be Mutah for the time while we were buddies. But she is Armenian."

Thomas was suspicious. "Mutah? I don't know that word."

"I am happy with that," the Governor said. "If the girl is happy, then the matter is resolved."

"Hang on," Thomas said. "It can't happen unless I know what it is that's happening."

The Governor laughed long and hard. "Rifleman, do you know of the phrase: 'A taste of your own medicine'? This is an auspicious start. You might ask your protected flower and get her to explain."

Thomas recognised a trap when he heard one. He would ask someone, but definitely not Abla. "Imam, would Mutah be honourable for Hayastan and Esmail?"

"They are both very young. Very, very young. Too young for full Mutah. That aside, it would avoid any appearance of dishonour."

"But what does it mean?"

The Governor laughed again.

*****

Frank felt uneasy. He checked on his Section, to make sure everyone was fine and that they had everything they needed. He wasn't entirely sure what was bothering him, but he was sure something wasn't right.

He went to speak with Sergeant Taylor. Sergeant Taylor nodded sagely. "Sometimes, lad, you get these feelings. Sometimes they come to nothing and sometimes there's something behind them. You've got to make sure everyone's ready without causing panic. Surprise inspections are always a good standby, but not here. It will disturb the locals. I've had the same feeling here, so let's go around, check on everyone, make sure we're ready for anything. And keep your eyes open for anything that feels wrong."

*****

Thomas introduced Hayastan and Esmail to each other. They were very suspicious and wary of each other at first.

"I am the Corporal of the mascots," Hayastan said.

"And I'm a son of the Governor."

"You're a rifleman mascot now. You're a mascot and I'm a mascot corporal."

Thomas let them bicker for a while. As they did so, they spoke faster and faster. His Persian wasn't good enough to keep up with what they were saying. After a moment, he heard Esmail say the word Mutah, and Hayastan was surprised and suddenly stopped talking.

"What is Mutah?" Thomas asked.

"You are asking me for Mutah?" Hayastan said to Esmail. She still sounded surprised.

"What is Mutah?" Thomas asked again.

"We are to be comrades and buddies. Mutah, while we are comrades and buddies, will avoid any dishonour."

"What is Mutah?" Thomas asked yet again.

"Esmail, you do know that I'm an Armenian?"

"What is Mutah?" Thomas was starting to get annoyed.

"No," said Esmail thoughtfully. "You are a rifleman mascot, and I am a rifleman mascot."

"No. You are a rifleman mascot, and I am a rifleman mascot corporal."

"If you don't tell me what Mutah is, neither of you will be riflemen."

"Mutah, it's, well, it's Mutah," Esmail explained.

Hayastan also seemed at a loss how to explain. "It would be for while we were both riflemen."

"Riflemen mascots," Thomas said with a sigh.

"Unless we become real riflemen," Hayastan corrected. "And I'm a rifleman mascot corporal."

"Mutah. What is it?" Thomas practically shouted.

Both Esmail and Hayastan looked surprised. Esmail spoke carefully. "When a man and a woman are alone together, they must either be relatives or married. We are not relatives, but we cannot be married. So, Mutah."

Thomas frowned. That was one question sort of answered, several others raised. "You're twelve. She's seven. You're not a man and she's not a woman."

"But who knows when we will be? Mutah avoids dishonour."

"So Mutah is marriage?"

"No!" said Esmail and Hayastan at the same time, then they looked at each other in distaste.

"It's not marriage," Esmail explained. "Marriage is when man and woman marry."

"Mutah is when a man and a woman marry," Hayastan added.

"What is the difference?" Thomas was trying to keep his temper in check. They were obviously trying to explain, but this was getting silly.

"Marriage is when you get married, and it lasts until Allah separates you," said Esmail.

"Mutah is when you decide how long you will be married for. Sometimes for three years, sometimes just for an hour. I don't know why anyone would want to be married for an hour. That's silly."

"So Mutah is a temporary marriage."

"Well, sort of."

Thomas was glad that he hadn't asked Abla what it was. He could see that there might have been misunderstandings.

*****

In the morning, Davie started to show Lintonga to Esmail and Hayastan. He used two sticks to defend himself while they both tried to attack him. Abla watched them, making sure that the two children didn't get hurt. There would be a time when she had her own children to look after.

It seemed unnecessary, as they were full of energy and Davie was making sure he only defended and didn't attack. They'd worked out that they should attack from different directions.

The other Zulus watched as well, and busily and loudly gave both helpful and unhelpful advice.

Thomas watched, wondering how the Persian religion could have such strange rules about marriage. Child marriage was the sort of thing you read about in history books. As for temporary marriages, well, that was just weird. A thought crossed his mind. Being married to Emily on Mondays and Thursdays, to Abla on Tuesdays and Fridays, and to Joy on Wednesdays and Saturdays. "Sunday would be my day of rest."

A few minutes later, he wondered what he was doing daydreaming about being married to Joy.

When the children were exhausted, Abla picked up the sticks. "May I speak with Rifleman Davie?" she asked Thomas. Thomas nodded, puzzled.

"Abla fought alongside her hero and her husband in the tales," she said to Davie. "I need to be prepared to do the same if I am to be worthy. Teach me how it is done."

"One stick to attack, one to defend," Davie said, indulgently. The other Zulus jeered at him for fighting women and children. He jeered back, saying that women and children were more of a contest for him than they were.

Davie and Abla started to fight. Within seconds, Davie had been hit on the wrist, and his gentle return blow hit thin air as Abla stepped out of reach. He stared at her, and she looked at the ground in embarrassment.

"I apologise. It is not my place to harm you."

"Harm me? That little tap? I was taken by surprise."

The Zulus laughed fit to burst. Davie settled down to start again, this time paying more attention. The contest fell into a pattern; Abla would dance in, strike at Davie a couple of times, most of which were blocked, then danced out of range before he attacked. When she did land a blow, it sounded like she was hitting a lump of teak, and it had about as much effect. He couldn't hit her, but after a while, she started to slow down, and he manoeuvred the fight onto uneven ground. After a few more minutes, Abla was breathing heavily, then Davie stopped.

"That is enough lesson for the time being. I now have duties I must attend to. Some other time, I'll teach you more."

The other Zulus jeered about who would be teaching whom, and added some rather earthy comments about what the lessons might involve. Luckily, Abla had walked over to Thomas and didn't hear the comments.

"I must go to my uncle. He is expecting me. That was how Abla fought alongside her love."

"Wait, where do you learn to fight like that?"

"Dancing lessons," Abla replied. "My uncle said that as my father did not acknowledge my existence, I would need dancing lessons to protect my honour."

Thomas shook his head as he watched her leave. He'd have to be careful at the next Regimental dance.

Davie also watched Abla walk away, his eyes fixed on her graceful movement.

*****

"O'Grady, stop wool-gathering. Lieutenant Hawkins wants you. Now." Sergeant Taylor was not bothering to hide the urgency in his voice, which told Thomas all he needed to know about the situation. He walked briskly with Sergeant Taylor across the square to a corner, where Lieutenant Hawkins was talking to a Persian cavalry officer.

As he got closer, Thomas recognised him as the one who they'd met out on patrol. He looked exhausted and scared.

"O'Grady, come here. Colonel Mofakham has news, and I need to know exactly what he's saying. No misunderstandings."

The Colonel looked worried rather than scared. Anxious and excited. He spoke rapidly, switching between bad English and rapid Persian.

"Slower, please, Sir," Thomas said. He listened carefully. He understood the words, but they didn't make much sense. He questioned him to get confirmation what was being said. Finally, he turned to Lieutenant Hawkins.

"He said that the American came to their camp last night. He spoke with the Prince and the senior officers. This morning, they had all left, along with the elite infantry company. No-one knows where they've gone, and they left no orders. They also didn't leave any money, and the troops haven't been paid for a very long time. The troops are refusing to obey the officers who were still there, and one officer was murdered because he gave hard orders. The officers have, well, sir, he said the officers have run away. The men are angry, and he wants us to sort things out."

"Damn. Sergeant Taylor, get the men fallen in. Fully equipped."

"Sir?" asked Thomas.

"O'Grady. Those men haven't been paid for at least a year. There are no officers controlling them. They are about two thousand strong, armed. The richest man in the province is the Governor, and he's in that building there. This market square is the richest concentration of loot in the province. When they figure that out, they'll come. Get to your Section. Oh, O'Grady."

"Sir?"

"If you know any prayers, now might be a good time."

*****

The tone in Sergeant Taylor's voice as he got the riflemen formed up told everyone that this wasn't a simple exercise. No-one knew exactly what was going on, but there was an added urgency to everything. Once they got into line, Sergeant Taylor spoke to calm things down.

"Remember your drills and everything will be fine. Check your buddy's equipment. Make sure your water bottles are full. O'Grady?"

"Mascots, Sergeant. Get them out of the way?"

Hayastan and Esmail shook their heads. "We are riflemen. We will help. We'll bring water and magazines."

"It's going to be no place for children," Sergeant Taylor said.

"If you send us away," Esmail said, "you'll have to send a rifleman with us to stop us coming back. We can help."

Hayastan nodded fiercely in agreement.

"This is going to be no place for children. Or for women, Miss." This last he said to Abla.

"Sergeant, Abla fought alongside her hero. I shall do the same. What I shall do is keep these children safe and enable you to fight, if fight there is to be."

Sergeant Taylor sighed. He didn't have time to argue. "We're not going to stop you, are we, Miss. Make sure you keep out of our way, make sure the kids stay out of our way, and whatever you do, don't get between the men and the enemy. Blocks our field of fire. And if you get told to run, you take the kids and run, without any questions."

"I will keep the mascots safe," Abla said, taking the children to one side.

"O'Grady," Sergeant Taylor said. "I think your problems will start when the Regiment arrives."

Thomas was inclined to agree with him.

Lieutenant Campbell came across. "O'Grady. The Governor needs to be told what's going on. He's not going to pay attention to a child or a woman, so you need to tell him. Tell him to stay safe inside, his guards can look after him, then you come back. Quick as you can. Don't stop to charm yet another Persian lovely."

It was so unfair, Thomas thought as he hurried across. It wasn't his fault. Not that anyone believed him.

"Is there a problem?" the Governor had asked.

"There might very well be." Thomas explained the situation.

"And what will your group of soldiers be doing?"

"We'll be out there," Thomas said, baffled by the question. "That's what we're here for."

"And if things get bad? In which direction will you be retreating?"

"Retreat, Sir? We're here to stop this sort of thing, not run away from it. People under our protection get our protection."

The funny thing was, he meant it. He puzzled over this as he returned to report to Lieutenant Hawkins.

"Governor's been told, Sir. Mayor and Imam were with him." Thomas saw that the Persian officer was still here. "Sir?"

"God knows, O'Grady. Sort it out. Tell him he's done his job and he can go home, because I can't get through to him."

Thomas explained to the Persian Colonel. The Colonel took off his spectacles and cleaned them on a cloth before answering.

"I never wanted to join the Army, but it was decreed that I should. I am not a very good officer. My men ignore me. I get lost and I don't know what to do in the field. I am not very good at fighting. I would prefer to read, or play chess, or play bridge. I am scared. However, I am here, and my duty is to protect these people from bandits. I didn't think that my men would be the bandits, but that is the way things are. Whether I live or die here is in the hands of Allah, but I would rather die here with honour than live elsewhere without it."

"Well?" Lieutenant Hawkins asked. "What did he say?"

"He said he's staying, Sir. He said he might be able to talk sense into them. Probably not, but he thinks it worth trying."

"Tell him to keep out of our lines of fire."

Then it was quiet. Minutes turned into an hour, then two. The bazaar continued to operate, although the traders to the north end moved nearer to the centre.

No-one asked if it was a false alarm, though. Everyone could sense that something was about to happen. Lieutenant Hawkins walked from section to section, telling everyone what was happening. Two sections were at a wall, about half-way up the square, one section against the east wall, one against the west. A section was placed about fifty yards to the south of the sections against the wall, each about halfway to the centre of the square. Thomas' section was right in the middle of the square, forming the centre point of a W.

Lieutenant Hawkins finally took position with this section.

"Hurry up and wait," said Peter. "Always the way."

"Still think making off with the Prince's harem is such a bad idea?" Windy asked.

"Smoke if you've got them," Lieutenant Hawkins said. "If you've got them, why haven't you offered me one?" He stood in the centre of the Section, almost smiling and at ease. This was what he knew how to do. No more trying to understand diplomatic niceties or foreign ways.

"When the Persians arrive, that's the entrance they'll use," he said, pointing to the empty northern half of the square. "It's the closest to their base and they'll be thinking about loot and not expecting any problems. They'll take a while to get themselves sorted out. No officers, no-one any idea what's going on. They'll all want to do different things. Some will want to sit tight, some will want to go home, some will come here looting, some into the countryside to loot. They'll bicker and argue and then they'll each do their own thing by squad and section and platoon. They'll set off in dribs and drabs. There's around two thousand of them in total. We can reckon on half of them not coming here at all, and those that do come will arrive piecemeal."

"Wish the rest of the Regiment was here, Sir," said Windy.

Lieutenant Hawkins sighed. "O'Grady, I can't be bothered with the Crispin Day speech. You do it."

"Yes, Sir. We're here. The rest aren't. There's a job to be done. Shut up and get on with it. That's the short version, Sir."

"It'll do, O'Grady. When they come through those gates, they'll have the sun in their eyes. If they advance, they'll shy away from us and try and go into those two pockets to try and hit us in the flank. Those pockets are kill zones. Whichever way they turn, three sections will have lines of fire on them. They don't know how effective these rifles are over that range and they'll find out the hard way."

"Looks like we'll find out, Sir," said Peter. A file of cavalry rode in through the northern passageway and stopped a little way in. A dozen riders who they stopped and looked confused.

"Stay with the Section," said Frank. "Don't get separated."

Thomas glanced around. The other sections were in position and waiting. Behind them, Abla was with the two children, who had built up a pile of water bottles. The Imam was walking up to the Section.

Frank got the section to turn over traders' tables to form some impromptu cover. He thought it would be needed.

"Tell them to go back to barracks," Lieutenant Hawkins said to the Persian Colonel.

Another cavalry file rode into the square, bumping into the first, and they shouted at each other.

"They are not themselves," the Colonel said.

The Imam started to walk forward, clearly intent on talking to the troopers.

"Damn fool," said Lieutenant Hawkins. "I'll fetch him back. Keep them steady, Corporal." He walked briskly to catch up with the Imam, who had stopped and was talking to the nearest troopers.

"What's he saying?" Frank asked.

"Basically, God doesn't approve of violence here, and they should go home."

The troopers milled about, shouting at each other. They pointed at the bazaar, where traders were scooping up their goods and packing up as much as they could. The troopers pointed at the Imam, who stood still. They pointed at the building where the Governor was. For some reason, some of them pointed at the sky.

"They're drunk," said Peter.

"I don't think it's drink," Thomas said slowly. "We need to get Hawk and the Imam back."

He'd no sooner said the words than one of the troopers galloped his horse towards the Imam, waving his sword. Lieutenant Hawkins stepped between them, blocking the attempted blow with a rifle. This sparked the other troopers into action, who rode at the two. Lieutenant Hawkins shouted at the Imam to get clear as he tried to protect him.

As the horsemen closed, Frank gave the order to fire. Several riders were knocked from their saddles; the other sections fired, more Persian soldiers arrived through the archways, the horsemen rode past and over first Lieutenant Hawkins and then the Imam, slashing as they went. The three lead sections continued to fire.

The shock of the initial firing drove the cavalry back. They retreated into the troops arriving, causing confusion. The Zulus started to move forward, clambering over the overturned tables being used as cover. Frank bellowed at them to stay with the section.

"We stay together, strong like a fist. Separate, weak like fingers."

"You've obviously never been slapped by a lady," said Thomas, to some laughter.

"No," said Frank sharply. "You obviously have." This resulted in more laughter. Frank turned to the Persian Colonel. "Your job, keep eye on what happen to left and right. Warn us of trouble."

The Persian cavalry had increasing difficulties. The horses became harder and harder to control, disrupting everything. Thomas wondered if this was the time to advance and drive them out, but the feeling passed quickly.

The cavalry dismounted, crowding behind the infantry, pushing them forward.

The Riflemen opened fire again and the Persian infantry tried to halt to return fire, while being crowded and pushed forward by the press from those behind them trying to get forward.

Bullets started whipping in towards the Riflemen, kicking up dust and sending splinters firing from where they hit overturned tables.

Thomas focused. Pick a target. Breath out. Settle on the target. Squeeze the trigger. Hold the position for a count of two. Pick another target.

The infantry shied away from the centre and into the kill zone, but more were coming behind them. A last shot, then he had to take a step back to force them to clamber over the table, to catch them with the bayonet while they were off balance.

The sound was deafening. Rippling gunfire; shouts and screams and incoherent noise. Dust and smell. It was getting impossible to think. Thomas had to take a step backwards to avoid getting skewered. Out of the corner of his eye he caught the sight of a green jacket going down. No-one seemed to notice.

Then suddenly the Persians just turned and ran back. The sun was beating down and he was burning hot. A small hand thrust a water bottle at him, and he drank half of it and emptied the rest over his head before realising it was Hayastan who had handed it to him.

"Get the hell back out of things."

"Water first," she said. "That's my job."

"Your job is to stay safe."

"If you give me back the bottle quickly, I'll get back quicker."

There wasn't time to argue. "Just get back." He saw Esmail and Abla also helping, and he swore. Lieutenant Hawkins would create hell over civilians getting caught up in this.

No, he wouldn't. Lieutenant Hawkins was out there, next to the Imam.

Damn.

He heard Frank shouting his name and pointing at one of the Zulu riflemen lying on the ground. Thomas ran over and looked. Rifleman Charlie, bullet to the chest. Gone.

He found he'd got a wound on his wrist, and he had no memory of how he'd got that. It wasn't bad.

"Why aren't they going somewhere that's easier?" Windy asked.

"Because behind us is the biggest pay day they've ever known. That and they're drunk and not thinking straight."

"Stand to," shouted Frank.

The Persians came again, this time with snipers trying to keep the Riflemen from firing. Not that the snipers were any good, but they kept the riflemen from getting into a rhythm.

Then it was hand to hand, and everything became a blur. He glanced and saw that one of the sections had gone onto the roof tops to keep the snipers quiet. He could see that there was some fighting going on up there. He could sense a change in the atmosphere behind him. There was anger brewing, and he had no idea what that was about.

"Message from Lieutenant Campbell," said the Persian Colonel. "I might not be able to fight much, but I can run," he said, seeing Thomas' look of confusion. "He said the next time they come, when they get to within ten yards, this section is to pull back two hundred yards as fast as it can. Form a V and not a W."

"You should tell Corporal Barry."

"Language problems. Have to make sure the message is understood." He ran off, faster than Thomas had expected, weaving to avoid sniper fire, although there wasn't a great deal of that. He told Frank the instruction.

Thomas wasn't sure how it had happened, but somehow it had gone from mid-morning to mid-afternoon. He checked how everyone in the Section was. Abe had a wounded leg and Frank told him to get back to the new position. Abe argued.

"When we leave, we have to run. You can't run. You go now."

Abe scowled and started to argue, but Frank pointed. Abe reluctantly went.

Everyone, apart from Charlie, had scratches and minor wounds. Thomas wondered how the other sections were faring.

"Frank, when we retreat, there's going to be bullets following us. If anyone gets hit, they've got a problem. What do we do if anyone gets hit?"

Frank thought. This was a tough one. "You and Davie come in last. If anyone go down, you pick them up and carry them." He knew the risk that involved. "Windy and Peter, they first back, they give cover fire to you."

The Persian soldiers stood at the north end arguing.

"They're trying to work out if it's worth it," Peter said.

Thomas felt an atmosphere building up. Somehow, the bodies of Lieutenant Hawkins and the Imam had been recovered and taken to the rear. He didn't know when or how that happened, but he'd missed so much of what was going on.

Firing started again, and the Persians came forward again.

"Final hand," Thomas said. "Let's see what cards they've got."

No sooner than he had said the words than he felt a thump against his arm, sending a shot wild, and something warm hit the side and back of his head. He put his hand to the back of his neck, and his fingers felt sticky, and he saw blood on them, but he'd felt nothing. Then he saw Edward slumped across the table, the top of his head missing.

"Five rounds independent fire, then pull back to the packs. Pull back at the run."

"Don't try to walk backwards, just run," Thomas added. "You don't want to trip over."

Pick a target, squeeze the trigger, wait, move to the next. It was routine. Four rounds. Three. Two. One. Hold the last one while the others start pulling back. Zero, and turn.

Firing from the sections to the side kept the Persians back, a little. Davie was level with him. Thomas got the impression that Davie could have gone faster but was staying alongside Thomas. Bullets whipped past them. Good luck with hitting a moving target while you're running, Thomas thought.

Windy stumbled and dropped to his knees, blood soaking into his trousers. Davie grabbed him under one arm, Thomas grabbed him under the other arm, and they half-ran, half-staggered to the packs where the others were providing covering fire.

"I've got him," said Peter. "My shoulder's out, can't shoot."

"Stop the bleeding," Thomas said. "You'll probably need a tourniquet."

"I'll help," said Abla.

Thomas wanted to shout at her that this was no place for a woman to be, but there wasn't time. Hayastan and Esmail were also by the packs, keeping low and looking scared, flinching at the sounds of the rifles, but handing things to Abla as she asked for them.

No time, turn to face the Persians.

*****

Peter sliced at Windy's trouser leg with a knife, and exposed a long, deep wound freely pumping blood. It seemed to have missed the big blood vessels, but Windy looked very pale.

"Not a problem," Peter said. "I'll just tie this up, then you can get treated by Nurse Charrington when the Regiment gets here."

"I'll do that," Windy said weakly, trying to push Peter aside.

"Lad, if you're worrying about your secret coming out, I've known since you got drunk in London and I had to put you to bed. I'll tie this up, Nurse Charrington will stitch it up and no-one will be any the wiser."

"You've known?"

"Of course I have. I'm not a complete idiot. Do you think I'm going to shop my buddy?"

Windy started to lose consciousness, and Peter could hear fighting behind him. "You," he said, pointing at Esmail. "Hold this here, tight. Tighto, understando?" He pointed at Hayastan. "You, keep him awake. No sleepo. Understando?"

He stood up and as he turned around, a Persian soldier thrust a bayonet at him, taking him square in the stomach. He crumpled to the ground, clutching at the rifle. The Persian tried to recover his rifle, then crumpled himself as a rifle butt hit him on the side of the head.

Abla reversed the rifle and stood by the packs. "You do as you were told," she said to the children. "Esmail keep the bleeding stopped, Hayastan, keep the soldier awake. I shall guard you." She wished she wasn't so scared and that she wasn't shaking so much, but if Abla fought alongside her love, then she had to also. She looked at Windy, puzzled.

*****

Some had reached them, and it was bayonet work again. The soldiers facing them weren't keen to be the first to close. Davie wanted to take the fight to them. Charge them and they would flee. Corporal Barry said that they were to stick together and hold position.

There was a scream from behind him, and Davie glanced, and saw Abla knocking an enemy to the ground, with another Persian warily approaching her.

"Behind us. I've got this," he shouted to Thomas. Davie then rushed over and stabbed the Persian with all his strength.

"*Shiya umkami wedwa. Usuthu.*" Twist and withdraw and look around to see if there were any more. He realised what he'd said, leave my woman alone, and hoped no-one had noticed. Abla nodded and indicated one side while she turned to watch the other side. For a moment, they stood back-to-back, looking around for any enemy, but there were none in sight.

He looked back up the market square and the Persians were pulling back. They were being pelted with stones from local people as they went. Then the Persians were no longer pulling back, but were running, all order gone.

"Check your rifles," ordered Corporal Barry.

*****

Lieutenant Campbell tried to mop his brow and found it hard. His hand was shaking uncontrollably. He couldn't let the men see. He had to try and clear his brain. What did he have to do now? Check on the men, check on the situation. His mind was fuzzy and there was a lot to remember that he had to do.

The Persians were fleeing, and the citizens threw rocks after them as they fled. The citizens were angry. Probably because the Persians had killed the Imam. That was probably a bad thing.

First, he had to check on the men. He was just so exhausted.

"How do we stand, Sergeant?" Lieutenant Campbell tried to keep the exhaustion out of his voice.

"Seven dead, including Lieutenant Hawkins. Eight wounded. Black Section got hit the hardest. Three dead, two wounded. That was to be expected. Lieutenant Hawkins put them in the centre. Best place for them. Best hand-to-hand section in the platoon, worst at rifle fire. Put them where they'll do the most fighting and give the other sections longer at shooting. They were always going to get the worst of it, Sir." Sergeant Taylor stood stiffly, with an occasional glance to the line of blanket-covered figures. Now, more than ever, he had to hold it together and he had to make sure Lieutenant Campbell did as well. He could grieve for Lieutenant Hawkins later. The living come first.

"Will our wounded get back into the ranks?"

"Six will, eventually. Rifleman Walsh might, if the doc can fix his shoulder up. Corporal Wilson's lost a leg at the knee. No chance for him."

"The dead?" Lieutenant Campbell hated asking the question, but it had to be asked.

"Lieutenant Hawkins, Sir. Corporal Furtek, Section One. Riflemen Tomkins and Brown, Section Two. Riflemen Grant, Charlie, and Edward, Black Section."

"I think they've earned the right to be called Section Five, Sergeant. It looks like the Governor wants a word with me. Get O'Grady over here. Post pickets, then let the rest of the men sleep."

"Yes, Sir. Sir, the men expect you to calm them down. Be your normal self, Sir. If you aren't, they'll worry."

"Bright-eyed and bushy-tailed like a border collie? I don't think I've got it in me at the moment."

"Yes, you have, Sir. It's your job. You're in charge, Sir, so you've got it in you, whether you have or not."

"I'm so tired, Sergeant."

"Perks of being an officer, Sir. You're not allowed to be tired. It's in Regulations."

*****

Windy pushed Abla away. "I'm bandaged. I'm not bleeding. The doctor is busy. Nurse Charrington will be along and she can stitch up anything that needs stitching up. I can't stand guard, but I can sit guard. I'm going to say goodbye to Peter, OK? Thanks to him and thanks to the children, I get to keep my leg. What's Persian for Thank you? Now leave me be."

*****

Esmail tried to hold back the tears. "I am a coward," he said to Thomas. "I was so scared."

Thomas bent down at the knee to come down to Esmail's level. "Being scared means you were brave, not a coward."

"I don't understand."

"You're not scared when you're drinking tea. There's no bravery in drinking tea. It's when you're scared that you get to show how brave you are. Courage is when you're scared to do something, but do it anyway, because it has got to be done. Do you think I wasn't scared?"

"So, it's not shameful to be scared?"

"Everyone gets scared. It's how you handle being scared that matters."

*****

Sergeant Taylor walked across to where Frank stood, near the line of blanketed figures.

"It's hard, lad. It was especially hard for you. You're thinking that you let them down, that if you'd done something different, something better, they'd still be here. You were always going to get it rough, and you kept your boys together. When it comes to it, all you can do is make sure your boys are as well-prepared as they can be, that you've shifted the odds in their favour as much as you can, that you keep them focused. Then it's down to fate."

"Was there something else I could have done?"

"You got them through a tough spot. Officer down, outnumbered, raw troops, and your blacks aren't up to Rifle standards yet. They've not had the time. Civilians to worry about and tough lines of retreat. You got thrown in the deep end. If you'd done badly, you wouldn't be worrying, because every last one of you would be under a blanket. I've known experienced NCOs who wouldn't have done so well. What do you do next?"

"Post pickets. That done. Check the wounded. Make them comfortable. See they've got best help. Get them better. Check the lightly wounded. Get them comfortable. Then check with Lieutenant Campbell for further orders."

"Well done, lad. Very well done."

*****

The Governor came out and walked slowly across to the platoon. He spoke first with his son, rapidly and apart from the others. Esmail hugged his father, then stood up straight. Esmail went to Hayastan, and the Governor came across to where Lieutenant Campbell and Thomas were waiting for him.

"Young man, you spoke truly when you said you would stay. I wasn't sure that you would, but you did. This isn't your home, Lieutenant. Why did you fight so hard for it?"

"Governor," said Lieutenant Campbell. "That wasn't fighting hard." Thomas could tell the Lieutenant was trying to be jocular, but it hit a false note. The Governor's eyes flicked momentarily towards the line of blanketed bodies.

"I think I understand," he said. "For civilians and for people unfamiliar with this, it seemed fierce and confusing. I think those who came would say likewise. What did they lose here?"

Lieutenant Campbell glanced at Thomas.

"They had thirty-two dead, Sir."

"Wounded?" Lieutenant Campbell asked.

"They had no wounded, Sir."

"They must have had some, O'Grady."

"No, Sir. The citizens took care of the wounded. They were upset that their Imam had been murdered. No wounded, Sir."

Lieutenant Campbell flinched at this.

"They killed an Imam," the Governor said, almost gently. "A teacher, a man of God, a man of peace. They've been disturbing trading for months, stealing and looting and carrying off women. Purses have been emptied and daughters filled. Mercy was never going to happen.

"I have to thank you and your brave men for what they have done. It's not yet finished, I know, but I doubt those soldiers will trouble the city again. The villages, they will still need protection from the real bandits and the army bandits, but your people have started well. You have our thanks, and your sacrifices here mean that you are our honoured guests. Although I expect the traders here will still strike hard bargains with you."

"Your son was very brave," Lieutenant Campbell said. "A boy to be proud of."

"He has said that he would like to stay with you for your stay. It is an unusual boarding school, but I suspect he will learn to be a man. If he grows up to be a man who does right even when it is at some risk, and when not doing right would be easy, then he would be a man I would be happy to have as a son."

"Colonel Dalkeith will have to confirm, obviously."

"Thank you, Sir," Thomas said quickly. "Lieutenant, you told me to remind you that we need to do a circuit to check for security." He had to drag Lieutenant Campbell away before he made any commitments.

"I would like to thank you men personally," said the Governor. "With your permission."

Damn. He's good, thought Thomas. If we stay with him, he gets agreements from Lieutenant Campbell. If we don't, he gets the men seeing him as the Persian authority, not the King. He wins, either way.

"By all means," said Lieutenant Campbell. Once the Governor was out of earshot, he turned to Thomas. "Your point?"

"He's a politician, Sir. You're not. He wants commitments from us to support his position. When I was with him when he was talking with Lieutenant Hawkins, we learned that there's some sort of politics going on between him and the King. We really don't want to get caught up in that, Sir."

"Thank you, O'Grady. If I were in your position, I don't know what would worry me more; the fact that you seem to understand politicians suspiciously well, or the fact that you don't seem to understand your own officers. I'm not going to make any agreements about anything with Colonel Dalkeith arriving tomorrow. I've a report to write. While I'm doing that, see if there is a telegraph line to the railway stations. If there is, have this message sent, so that Colonel Dalkeith has some advance warning." He handed a slip of paper to Thomas.

*****

Thomas scowled as he looked around the bazaar. That doctor was busy looking at the wounded, displaying the kind of medical dedication that Emily would admire.

The thought scared him. He knew he wasn't thinking straight at the moment, but he wanted …

He wasn't sure what he wanted. He loved Emily, but Abla needed him. She'd lost her uncle and had no-one to protect her and she was as brave as a lion. Lioness. She was good with the children. Thomas felt totally confused.

He saw Abla talking with Windy. She seemed to be sympathetic towards him, gentle. Then he had a brilliant idea.

Windy had just lost his buddy and needed someone kind and gentle to help him through it. He was a lady's man, to judge from all that had been said about Beryl and Iris and a host of others. He needed someone more stable in his life right now. Abla had just lost her uncle and needed someone who she could devote her attentions to, someone who would be sympathetic and protective.

What was more, it didn't need to be permanent. Mutah, maybe for six months and then see how they'd hit it off. It was a perfect solution, flawless.

He would have to be careful how he explained it to them. Abla might assume he meant him, and Windy might feel like his wings were being clipped, but they were perfectly matched.

He'd let them get rested, everyone needed sleep. First thing in the morning, he would start putting the wheels in motion. Davie was keeping an eye on everyone, especially Abla and the two children. He'd been an absolute rock. Bit rash and he needed keeping in check, but he'd proved his worth.

He asked Abla if there were telegraphs at the stations. She said that there were, and they went to send the message to Colonel Dalkeith.

"My uncle has many letters," she said, slowly. "I think that you need to read them."

"That sounds very much like come up and see my etchings," Thomas said cheerfully. She didn't understand. "Actually, I've got something I need to talk about with you."

They went to her uncle's home, and she let him go in first. She offered him tea, her voice shaking. Then she started crying and once she started, she couldn't stop. He put his arms around her and let her cry.

*****

The train pulled up at a station. This was an unexpected, unscheduled stop, and Colonel Dalkeith knew that this meant bad news. Someone gave him a telegram slip. That was never good.

He read it and swore. That woke Lady Dalkeith.

"I need to speak with the company commanders and nurses."

It took a few moments to wake everybody up and get them to the Colonel's compartment. Four company commanders, four nurses, Joy, and the RN liaison officer crowded in. There wasn't room to move as the train started again.

"I've news from Esfahan. Captain Filleul, your company is excused unloading duties. The second we arrive at the station, you're to take your company, in battle order, straight to the city and report to Lieutenant Campbell, or whoever the senior man there is. The nurses will accompany you. We don't know what the situation will be, but it's been rough, so find out and get a report back as soon as you can."

"Yes, Sir. What do we know about the situation?"

"I received a telegram. It reads: "Heavy fighting. Situation stabilised. Ammunition low. Regimental support requested. Lieutenant Hawkins and six others dead, eight serious injuries." That's what we know. The fact that they've used the Esfahan telegraph suggests that the civilians there are cooperative. Gentleman, ladies, I believe you have preparations to make."

"Ladies, before you go, I'd like a word with you," said Lady Dalkeith. "Some of you have loved ones in Esfahan, and you're worried. Worry is inevitable. Support each other and remember that the better you do your job, the more likely your loved one will come through this. If you come across any news, let me know. If I've any news, good or bad, I will keep you informed."

"Please be safe, Thomas," whispered Emily. Joy and Alice had similar thoughts.

Read on for an extract from the next book in the series:

Arrows of Desire

Arrows of Desire

Abla finally stopped crying and rested in Thomas' arms. "I am sorry. My uncle, the day, everything. I should not be so weak."

Thomas held her to comfort her. He smelt jasmine, or something, in her hair. He was still on edge because of the events of the day and he stroked her hair. He looked down as she looked up and he felt emotion starting to take a hold.

"Be careful, Thomas." He could almost hear Emily's words.

That had been so close. So very close. He'd known desire before, but nothing like that. Thomas took a deep breath.

"With your uncle gone, I have to fill his place."

Abla looked up at him with big, brown eyes and held him close. "You are a man of great honour. I wish you to be my husband, not my uncle. I understand. You do not want disharmony in your household, so your first wife must be happy with my presence in your house. That is how it must be."

"Let's look at these letters." He had to do something, because if he didn't, well, he wasn't sure he would be able to control his urges. He started to read the letters and Abla sat uncomfortably close. Actually, it wasn't uncomfortable as such. It was very comfortable. That's what made it uncomfortable. The smell of her hair, the softness of her hand as their fingers touched turning the papers over, the warmth of her side against him, her foot touching his ankle.

"Abla, I've been thinking about Windy. He lost his buddy in the fighting." Thomas paused. Peter was gone. He'd never hear him complaining about the unfairness of the current system, how things were broken, and they had to be rebuilt and not just held together. He'd never have to sigh as Peter redistributed wealth to himself. He'd never hear his constant banter with Windy. Windy was going to be devastated.

Thomas felt tears welling up and Abla placed a hand on his shoulder. He had to fight temptation again. "Windy's lost his best friend. It would be good if you could keep an eye on him. Be his friend, someone he can talk to."

"Windy? But, Windy?" Her voice trailed off in confusion.

"As a favour. A good deed."

"I think I understand," she said slowly. "You want me to comfort Windy. Windy can teach me while you are busy. While I am being taught in the ways of the Regiment, my honour will not be compromised."

"Well, he's a good lad. I'm not sure your honour, no, he's a good lad. He understands women, which probably makes him the only soldier who does."

"I understand. Then, when all is settled, your first wife will be able to judge if I am worthy of you."

Explaining was proving to be difficult. Thomas suspected that it was because Abla didn't want to understand. The best thing to do would be to focus on the letters.

*****

Lady Dalkeith drew herself up. "Joy, there is nothing you can do. Corporal Barry is either safe or he is not safe. This is what being a soldier's wife involves. He relies on you to cope with everything here, even though you are worried sick with what might be happening where he is. If you cope, he will return, and the reunion is usually extremely passionate. If you do not cope, the reunion will be less satisfactory."

"Yes, Ma'am. Ma'am, what if?"

"You play the hand that you are dealt. That is all one can do. This is what being the wife of a soldier is. You wave goodbye and you're never sure they'll come back. Oh, and Joy."

"Yes, Ma'am?"

"Don't wear your best clothes when you see him first."

"But Ma'am, I'll want to look my best."

"He'll not be paying attention to your clothes."

*****

Everything was settled, the pickets posted, the wounded treated. He'd checked on ammunition and distributed what was left to those still able to use it. He'd done everything that he could.

Sergeant Taylor paused by the line of blankets. He had to hold himself together until the Regiment arrived, but he couldn't pass without stopping here for a moment.

"Turns out you went first, John. It's going to be strange here without you. You'd have been proud of our boys. They're not like we planned, but they've come together well. They stood and they have shown they can work well. They'll give us grey hairs yet, mind you. Still, we shall see. Tell Doris I still think of her. You two take care of each other until it's my turn to come over."

He straightened his shoulders. Time to get his mind back on to looking after the living.

*****

The letters were from other Imams, and they seemed fairly mundane. Thomas persevered with them. This was partly because the Persians respected Imams and knowing how they thought could be useful. Mainly, however, it was because he knew that if he stopped reading, he would end up seducing Alba. That could lead to complications.

The Imams were not happy. That was obvious from the start. Things were not going well, and they talked about their concerns to each other. Most of the Imams he wrote to were from towns in the province, but some were from further afield. Thomas read about physical difficulties, of bandits going unchecked, often aided and abetted by the Army. He read about projects started but unfinished through lack of money. Roads and schools and hospitals were in disarray because of a shortage of money, although people were taxed heavily and there seemed no shortage of money for giant statues.

The Imams complained that the provincial Governors lived in luxury. They'd sent a delegation to the Governor of this province. The letters said he had promised to ensure that the province prospered. He promised to deal with the bandits, he promised to find an army that will fight them and stop them. He promised to find a source of income to deal with poverty. He promised to apply fairly just laws. He had promised a lot. The Imams had warned that discontent was growing and that failure to deliver would be badly received. He proposed an airship port, the best between India and Egypt.

The letters talked about the King and the King's Court. Thomas was surprised at how openly critical the letters were. They complained about him trying to regain the glory days of the Peacock Throne. They complained about the licentiousness at the Court. They criticised the King specifically and unequivocally. "If he desires a woman, he takes her, whether she is married, promised, or maiden; whether her family agree or object; whether she is willing or not. He follows a simple rule: he desires, he takes."

The letters complained about foreigners. They said the British weren't to be trusted, because they supported the King and didn't care what happened, so long as the King gave them what they wanted. They said the Russians stirred up trouble on the border so they could move in to quell the trouble and get the border people used to Russian rule. The Turks were forcing their unwanted people into Persia, and the Germans delighted in causing disturbances and keeping them going.

Abla had fallen asleep, her head on his shoulder. Sound asleep. She'd had a long and tiring day. He picked her up very carefully, so as not to disturb her, and carried her to a bed. As he was laying her down, she murmured something in her sleep. Thomas couldn't quite make it out, but it sounded like: "I'm sorry, Uncle. The pretence has become the truth."

*****

Dawn arrived. With it came the first platoon of Captain Filleul's company. Lieutenant Campbell reported to Captain Filleul, summarising events. The rest of the company arrived, posted pickets, allowing the Scout platoon to relax. The citizens watched the new soldiers warily.

Shortly after, the nurses arrived and started to look at the wounded.

"With your permission, Sir," Alasdair said to Captain Filleul.

"She's working, remember. Just let her know you're safe, Reunion can wait."

"Of course, Sir." Alasdair bounced over and stood behind Alice as she checked on Rifleman Walsh. He waited quietly, until she stood up, then he moved close, and put his hands over her eyes.

"Three guesses."

She spun around and hugged him fiercely. "Alasdair, I was so worried."

"You got it in one. When we're both off-duty, I'll show you around the city."

"You're all right," she said, still holding him tightly, not wanting to let go.

"Of course. I missed all the rough stuff."

"Don't, Alasdair. I know you. You'll have done your best and you'll have done your duty. You'll have been in as much danger as anyone. Please don't try to lie to me to stop me worrying."

Alasdair bent down and kissed her on the forehead. "If I were to do more than that little kiss, well, the people here don't like having their horses scared. Alice, you'll *know* if anything happens to me. You get back to work, I'll get back to work. We'll explore the city together later."

"Is it safe? The city, I mean."

"Absolutely. Outside the city, not yet. But the people of the city, they like us."

Printed in Great Britain
by Amazon